CHILDREN OF THE NIGHT

CHILDREN OF THE NIGHT

Stories of Ghosts, Vampires, Werewolves, and "Lost Children"

CHILDREN OF THE NIGHT SERIES

Edited by Martin H. Greenberg

Cumberland House
Nashville, Tennessee

Published by Cumberland House Publishing, Inc., 431 Harding Industrial Drive, Nashville, TN 37211-3160.

Cover design by Becky Brauner
Interior design by Mike Towle

Library of Congress Cataloging-in-Publication data is available.
ISBN: 1-58182-037-2

Printed in the United States of America
1 2 3 4 5 6 7 — 03 02 01 00 99

CONTENTS

INTRODUCTION

In the minds of adults, childhood is usually sentimentally remembered as a happy, carefree time full of fun and laughter, and one of the few times when, except for certain parental limits, they possessed total freedom to explore the world. It was a time of endless curiosity and learning, with new wonders and experiences around every corner.

However, as some people may not be willing to acknowledge, childhood contained its own share of dangers. Unless one happened to be one of the "golden people" who floated through life doing no wrong, growing up was a bewildering array of choices, from how to dress to what friends to choose and groups to be with to peer pressure regarding drugs, alcohol, etc. Make the wrong choice, and a boy or girl would be ostracized from his or her peers, taunted mercilessly (and there is nothing like the calculated cruelty of children), and driven to depression, drug abuse, and perhaps even suicide.

For most parents, children are a living symbol of hope and promise for the future. After all, they think, my little Bobby or Jill could grow up to cure a disease, become a famous musician or performer, or perhaps (when the following would have been a source of pride) become the president of the United States. Many parents see their children as being able to make up for the mistakes or failures the parents themselves committed and may try to pressure their children into a certain career, not realizing the harm they may be doing. Children suffer under this sometimes unyielding pressure and, wanting to succeed to make their parents happy, often crack under the strain of trying to please.

Then there is the dark side of human nature that is also waiting to entrap children, from drug pushers to pedophiles to child pornographers. There is always someone, somewhere, waiting to use a boy or girl and throw them away.

Faced with all of this, one would think that children would have no hope of handling the dangers that inhabit the world around them. But that is where many people underestimate children. They have survived the worst that other human beings can throw at them, and they still keep going, becoming the adults who shape the future and, hopefully, prevent the cycle from happening again.

The children in the stories collected in this volume—whether good or evil; whether ghost, werewolf, or vampire; whether protecting themselves or others, like the girl in Charles de Lint's touching "There's No Such Thing," or maliciously out for themselves, as the child sorcerer is in Cyril M. Kornbluth's "The Words of Guru"—all have one thing in common: They all face problems and fears that only children endure. How they handle them may surprise you, but it befits them, because they are the children of the night . . .

CHILDREN OF THE NIGHT

BOOBS

Suzy McKee Charnas

T he thing is, it's like your brain wants to go on
thinking about the miserable history mid-term
you have to take tomorrow, but your body takes
over. And what a body! You can see in the dark and run
like the wind and leap parked cars in a single bound.

Of course you pay for it the next morning (but it's
worth it). I always wake up stiff and sore, with dirty
hands and feet and face, and I have to jump in the
shower fast so Hilda won't see me like that.

Not that she would know what it was about, but why
take chances? So I pretend it's the other thing that's
bothering me. So she goes, "Come on, sweetie, everybody gets cramps, that's no reason to go around moaning and groaning. What are you doing, trying to get out
of school just because you've got your period?"

If I didn't like Hilda, which I do even though she is only a stepmother instead of my real mother, I would show her something that would keep me out of school forever, and it's not fake, either.

But there are plenty of people I'd rather show that to.

I already showed that dork Billy Linden.

"Hey, Boobs!" he goes, in the hall right outside Homeroom. A lot of kids laughed, naturally, though Rita Frye called him an asshole.

Billy is the one that started it, sort of, because he always started everything, him with his big mouth. At the beginning of term, he came barreling down on me hollering, "Hey, look at Bornstein, something musta happened to her over the summer! What happened, Bornstein? Hey, everybody, look at Boobs Bornstein!"

He made a grab at my chest, and I socked him in the shoulder, and he punched me in the face, which made me dizzy and shocked and made me cry, too, in front of everybody.

I mean, I always used to wrestle and fight with the boys, being that I was strong for a girl. All of a sudden it was different. He hit me hard, to really hurt, and the shock sort of got me in the pit of my stomach and made me feel nauseous, too, as well as mad and embarrassed to death.

I had to go home with a bloody nose and lie with my head back and ice wrapped in a towel on my face and dripping down into my hair.

Hilda sat on the couch next to me and patted me. She goes, "I'm sorry about this, honey, but really, you have to learn it sometime. You're all growing up and the boys are getting stronger than you'll ever be. If you fight with boys, you're bound to get hurt. You have to find other ways to handle them."

To make things worse, the next morning I started to bleed down there, which Hilda had explained carefully to me a couple of times, so at least I knew what was going on. Hilda really tried extra hard without being icky about it, but I hated when she talked about how it was all part of these exciting changes in my body that are so important and how terrific it is to "become a young woman."

Sure. The whole thing was so messy and disgusting, worse than she had said, worse than I could imagine, with these black clots of gunk coming out in a smear of pink blood—I thought I would throw up. That's just the lining of your uterus, Hilda said. Big deal. It was still gross.

And, plus, the *smell*.

Hilda tried to make me feel better, she really did. She said we should "mark the occasion" like primitive people do, so it's something special, not just a nasty thing that just sort of falls on you.

So we decided to put poor old Pinkie away, my stuffed dog that I've slept with since I was three. Pinkie is bald and sort of hard and lumpy, since he got put in the washing machine by mistake, and you would never know he was all soft plush when he was new, or even that he was pink.

Last time my friend Gerry-Anne came over, before the summer, she saw Pinky laying on my pillow and though she didn't say anything, I could tell she was thinking that was kind of babyish. So I'd been thinking about not keeping Pinky around anymore.

Hilda and I made him this nice box lined with pretty scraps from her quilting class, and I thanked him out loud for being my friend for so many years, and we put him up in the closet, on the top shelf.

I felt terrible, but if Gerry-Anne decided I was too babyish to be friends with anymore, I could end up with no friends at all. When you have never been popular since the time you were skinny and fast and everybody wanted you on their team, you have that kind of thing on your mind.

Hilda and Dad made me go to school the next morning so nobody would think I was scared of Billy Linden (which I was) or that I would let him keep me away just by being such a dork.

Everybody kept sneaking funny looks at me and whispering, and I was sure it was because I couldn't help walking funny with the pad between my legs and because they could smell what was happening, which as far as I knew hadn't happened to anybody else in Eight A yet. Just like nobody else in the whole grade had anything real in their stupid training bras except me, thanks a lot.

Anyway I stayed away from everybody as much as I could and wouldn't talk to Gerry-Anne, even, because I was scared she would ask me why I walked funny and smelled bad.

Billy Linden avoided me just like everybody else, except one of his stupid buddies purposely bumped into me so I stumbled into Billy on the lunch-line. Billy turns around and he goes, real loud, "Hey, Boobs, when did you start wearing black and blue make-up?"

I didn't give him the satisfaction of knowing that he had actually broken my nose, which the doctor said. Good thing they don't have to bandage you up for that. Billy would be hollering up a storm about how I had my nose in a sling as well as my boobs.

That night I got up after I was supposed to be asleep and took off my underpants and T-shirt that I sleep in and stood looking at myself in the mirror. I didn't need to turn a light on. The moon was full and it was shining right into my bedroom through the big dormer window.

I crossed my arms and pinched myself hard to sort of punish my body for what it was doing to me.

As if that could make it stop.

No wonder Edie Siler had starved herself to death in the tenth grade! I understood her perfectly. She was trying to keep her body down, keep it normal-looking, thin and strong, like I was too, back when I looked like a person, not a cartoon that somebody would call "Boobs."

And then something warm trickled in a little line down the inside of my leg, and I knew it was blood and I couldn't stand it anymore. I pressed my thighs together and shut my eyes hard, and I did something.

I mean I felt it happening. I felt myself shrink down to a hard core of sort of cold fire inside my bones, and all the flesh part, the muscles and the squishy insides and the skin, went sort of glowing and free-floating, all shining with moonlight, and I felt a sort of shifting and balance-changing going on.

I thought I was fainting on account of my stupid period. So I turned around and threw myself on my bed, only by the time I hit it, I knew something was seriously wrong.

For one thing, my nose and my head were crammed with these crazy, rich sensations that it took me a second to even figure out were smells, they were so much stronger than any smells I'd ever smelled. And they were—I don't know—*interesting* instead of just stinky, even the rotten ones.

I opened my mouth to get the smells a little better, and heard myself panting in a funny way as if I'd been running, which I hadn't, and then there was this long part of my face sticking out and something moving there—my tongue.

I was licking my chops.

Well, there was this moment of complete and utter panic. I tore around the room whining and panting and hearing my toenails clicking on the floorboards, and then I huddled down and crouched in the corner because I was scared Dad and Hilda would hear me and come to find out what was making all this racket.

Because I could hear them. I could hear their bed creak when one of them turned over, and Dad's breath whistling a little in an almost snore, and I could smell them too, each one with a perfectly clear bunch of smells, kind of like those desserts of mixed ice cream they call a medley.

My body was twitching and jumping with fear and energy, and my room—it's a converted attic-space, wide but with a ceiling that's low in places—my room felt like a jail. And plus, I was terrified of catching a glimpse of myself in the mirror. I had a pretty good idea of what I would see, and I didn't want to see it.

Besides, I had to pee, and I couldn't face trying to deal with the toilet in the state I was in.

So I eased the bedroom door open with my shoulder and nearly fell down the stairs trying to work them with four legs and thinking about it, instead of letting my body just do it. I put my hands on the front door to open it, but my hands weren't hands, they were paws with long knobby toes covered with fur, and the toes had thick black claws sticking out of the ends of them.

The pit of my stomach sort of exploded with horror, and I yelled. It came out this wavery "wooo" noise that echoed eerily in my skullbones. Upstairs, Hilda goes, "Jack, what was that?" I bolted for the basement as I heard Dad hit the floor of their bedroom.

The basement door slips its latch all the time, so I just shoved it open and down I went, doing better on the stairs this time because I was too scared to think. I spent the rest of the night down there, moaning to myself (which meant whining through my nose, really) and trotting around rubbing against the walls trying to rub off this crazy shape I had, or just moving around because I couldn't sit still. The place was thick with stinks and these slow-swirling currents of hot and cold air. I couldn't handle all the input.

As for having to pee, in the end I managed to sort of hike my butt up over the edge of the slop-sink by Dad's workbench and let go in there. The only problem was that I couldn't turn the taps on to rinse out the smell because of my paws.

Then about three A.M. I woke up from a doze curled up in a bare place on the floor where the spiders weren't so likely to walk, and I couldn't see a thing or smell anything either, so I knew I was okay again even before I checked and found fingers on my hands again instead of claws.

I zipped upstairs and stood under the shower so long that Hilda yelled at me for using up the hot water when she had a load of wash to do that morning. I was only trying to steam some of the stiffness out of my muscles, but I couldn't tell her that.

It was real weird to just dress and go to school after a night like that. One good thing, I had stopped bleeding

after only one day, which Hilda said wasn't so strange for
the first time. So it had to be the huge greenish bruise on
my face from Billy's punch that everybody was staring at.

That and the usual thing, of course. Well, why not?
They didn't know I'd spent the night as a wolf.

So Fat Joey grabbed my book bag in the hallway
outside science class and tossed it to some kid from
Eight B. I had to run after them to get it back, which of
course was set up so the boys could cheer the jouncing
of my boobs under my shirt.

I was so mad I almost caught Fat Joey, except I was
afraid if I grabbed him, maybe he would sock me like
Billy had.

Dad had told me, Don't let it get you, kid, all boys
are jerks at that age.

Hilda had been saying all summer, Look, it doesn't
do any good to walk around all hunched up with your
arms crossed, you should just throw your shoulders back
and walk like a proud person who's pleased that she's
growing up. You're just a little early, that's all, and I bet
the other girls are secretly envious of you, with their cute
little training bras, for Chrissake, as if there was something that needed to be *trained.*

It's okay for her, she's not in school, she doesn't
remember what it's like.

So I quit running and walked after Joey until the
bell rang, and then I got my book bag back from the
bushes outside where he threw it. I was crying a little,
and I ducked into the girls' room.

Stacey Buhl was in there doing her lipstick like
usual and wouldn't talk to me like usual, but Rita came
bustling in and said somebody should off that dumb

dork Joey, except of course it was really Billy that put him up to it. Like usual.

Rita is okay except she's an outsider herself, being that her kid brother has AIDS, and lots of kids' parents don't think she should even be in the school. So I don't hang around with her a lot. I've got enough trouble, and anyway I was late for Math.

I had to talk to somebody, though. After school I told Gerry-Anne, who's been my best friend on and off since fourth grade. She was off at the moment, but I found her in the library and I told her I'd had a weird dream about being a wolf. She wants to be a psychiatrist like her mother, so of course she listened.

She told me I was nuts. That was a big help.

That night I made sure the back door wasn't exactly closed, and then I got in bed with no clothes on—imagine turning into a wolf in your underpants and T-shirt—and just shivered, waiting for something to happen.

The moon came up and shone in my window, and I changed again, just like before, which is not one bit like how it is in the movies—all struggling and screaming and bones snapping out with horrible cracking and tearing noises, just the way I guess you would imagine it to be, if you knew it had to be done by building special machines to do that for the camera and make it look real: if you were a special effects man, instead of a werewolf.

For me, it didn't have to look real, it was real. It was this melting and drifting thing, which I got sort of excited by it this time. I mean it felt—interesting. Like something I was doing, instead of just another dumb body-mess happening to me because some brainless hormones said so.

I must have made a noise. Hilda came upstairs to the door of my bedroom, but luckily she didn't come in. She's tall, and my ceiling is low for her, so she often talks to me from the landing.

Anyway I'd heard her coming, so I was in my bed with my whole head shoved under my pillow, praying frantically that nothing showed.

I could smell her, it was the wildest thing—her own smell, sort of sweaty but sweet, and then on top of it her perfume, like an ice-pick stuck in my nose. I didn't actually hear a word she said, I was too scared, and also I had this ripply shaking feeling inside me, a high that was only partly terror.

See, I realized all of a sudden, with this big blossom of surprise, that I didn't have to be scared of Hilda, or anybody. I was strong, my wolf-body was strong, and anyhow one clear look at me and she would drop dead.

What a relief, though, when she went away. I was dying to get out from under the weight of the covers, and besides I had to sneeze. Also I recognized that part of the energy roaring around inside me was hunger.

They went to bed—I heard their voices even in their bedroom, though not exactly what they said, which was fine. The words weren't important anymore, I could tell more from the tone of what they were saying.

Like I knew they were going to do it, and I was right. I could hear them messing around right through the walls, which was also something new, and I have never been so embarrassed in my life. I couldn't even put my hands over my ears, because my hands were paws.

So while I was waiting for them to go to sleep, I looked myself over in the big mirror on my closet door.

There was this big wolf head with a long slim muzzle and a thick ruff around my neck. The ruff stood up as I growled and backed up a little.

Which was silly of course, there was no wolf in the bedroom but me. But I was all strung out, I guess, and one wolf, me in my wolf body, was as much as I could handle the idea of, let alone two wolves, me and my reflection.

After that first shock, it was great. I kept turning one way and another for different views.

I was thin, with these long, slender legs but strong, you could see the muscles, and feet a little bigger than I would have picked. But I'll take four big feet over two big boobs any day.

My face was terrific, with jaggedy white ripsaw teeth and eyes that were small and clear and gleaming in the moonlight. The tail was a little bizarre, but I got used to it, and actually it had a nice plumy shape. My shoulders were big and covered with long, glossy-looking fur, and I had this neat coloring, dark on the back and a sort of melting silver on my front and under parts.

The thing was, though, my tongue, hanging out. I had a lot of trouble with that, it looked gross and silly at the same time. I mean, that was *my tongue*, about a foot long and neatly draped over the points of my bottom canines. That was when I realized that I didn't have a whole lot of expressions to use, not with that face, which was more like a mask.

But it was alive, it was my face, those were my own long black lips that my tongue licked.

No doubt about it, this was *me*. I was a werewolf, like in the movies they showed over Halloween weekend. But it wasn't anything like your ugly movie werewolf that's just some guy loaded up with pounds and pounds of make-up. I was *gorgeous.*

I didn't want to just hang around admiring myself in the mirror, though. I couldn't stand being cooped up in that stuffy, smell-crowded room.

When everything settled down and I could hear Dad and Hilda breathing the way they do when they're sleeping, I snuck out.

The dark wasn't very dark to me, and the cold felt sharp like vinegar, but not in a hurting way. Everyplace I went, there were these currents like waves in the air, and I could draw them in through my long wolf nose and roll the smell of them over the back of my tongue. It was like a whole different world, with bright sounds everywhere and rich, strong smells.

And I could run.

I started running because a car came by while I was sniffing at the garbage bags on the curb, and I was really scared of being seen in the headlights. So I took off down the dirt alley between our house and the Morrisons' next door, and holy cow, I could tear along with hardly a sound, I could jump their picket fence without even thinking about it. My back legs were like steel springs and I came down solid and square on four legs with almost no shock at all, let alone worrying about losing my balance or twisting an ankle.

Man, I could run through that chilly air all thick and moisty with smells, I could almost fly. It was like last year, when I didn't have boobs bouncing and yanking in front even when I'm only walking fast.

Just two rows of neat little bumps down the curve of my belly. I sat down and looked.

I tore open garbage bags to find out about the smells in them, but I didn't eat anything from them. I wasn't about to chow down on other people's stale hotdog-ends and pizza crusts and fat and bones scraped off their plates and all mixed in with mashed potatoes and stuff.

When I found places where dogs had stopped and made their mark, I squatted down and pissed there too, right on top, I just wiped them *out.*

I bounded across that enormous lawn around the Wanscombe place, where nobody but the Oriental gardener ever sets foot, and walked up the back and over the top of their BMW, leaving big fat pawprints all over it. Nobody saw me, nobody heard me, I was a shadow.

Well, except for the dogs, of course.

There was a lot of barking when I went by, real hysterics which at first I was really scared about. But then I popped out of an alley up on Ridge Road, where the big houses are, right in front of about six dogs that run together. Their owners let them out all night and don't care if they get hit by a car.

They'd been trotting along with the wind behind them, checking out all the garbage bags set out for pickup the next morning. When they saw me, one of them let out a yelp of surprise, and they all skidded to a stop.

Six of them. I was scared. I growled.

The dogs turned fast, banging into each other in their hurry, and trotted away.

I don't know what they would have done if they met a real wolf, but I was something special, I guess.

I followed them.

They scattered and ran.

Well, I ran too, and this was a different kind of running. I mean, I stretched, and I raced, and there was this joy. I chased one of them.

Zig, zag, this little terrier-kind of dog tried to cut left and dive under the gate of somebody's front walk, all without a sound—he was running too hard to yell, and I was happy running quiet.

Just before he could ooze under the gate, I caught up with him and without thinking I grabbed the back of his neck and pulled him off his feet and gave him a shake as hard as I could, from side to side.

I felt his neck crack, the sound vibrated through all the bones of my face.

I picked him up in my mouth, and it was like he hardly weighed a thing. I trotted away holding him up off the ground, and under a bush in Baker's Park held him down with my paws and I bit into his belly, that was still warm and quivering.

Like I said, I was hungry.

The blood gave me this rush like you wouldn't believe. I stood there a minute looking around and licking my lips, just sort of panting and tasting the taste because I was stunned by it, it was like eating honey or the best chocolate malted you ever had.

So I put my head down and chomped that little dog like shoving your face into a pizza and inhaling it. God, I was *starved*, so I didn't mind that the meat was tough and rank-tasting after that first wonderful bite. I even licked blood off the ground after, never mind the grit mixed in.

I ate two more dogs that night, one that was tied up on a clothesline in a cruddy yard full of rusted-out car parts down on the South side, and one fat old yellow dog out snuffling around on his own and way too slow.

He tasted pretty bad, and by then I was feeling full, so I left a lot.

I strolled around the park, shoving the swings with my big black wolf nose, and I found the bench where Mr. Granby sits and feeds the pigeons every day, never mind that nobody else wants the dirty birds around crapping on their cars. I took a dump there, right where he sits.

Then I gave the setting moon a goodnight, which came out quavery and wild, "Loo-loo-loo!" And I loped toward home, springing off the thick pads of my paws and letting my tongue loll out and feeling generally super.

I slipped inside and trotted upstairs, and in my room I stopped to look at myself in the mirror.

As gorgeous as before, and only a few dabs of blood on me, which I took time to lick off. I did get a little worried—I mean, suppose that was it, suppose having killed and eaten what I'd killed in my wolf shape, I was stuck in this shape forever? Like, if you wander into a fairy castle and eat or drink anything, that's it, you can't ever leave. Suppose when the morning came I didn't change back?

Well, there wasn't much I could do about that one way or the other, and to tell the truth, I felt like I wouldn't mind; it had been worth it.

When I was nice and clean, including licking off my own bottom which seemed like a perfectly normal and nice thing to do at the time, I jumped up on the bed, curled up, and corked right off. When I woke up with the sun in my eyes, there I was, my own self again.

It was very strange, grabbing breakfast and wearing my old sweatshirt that wallowed all over me so I didn't stick out so much, while Hilda yawned and shuffled around in her robe and slippers and acted like her and Dad hadn't been doing it last night, which I knew different.

And plus, it was perfectly clear that she didn't have a clue about what *I* had been doing, which gave me a strange feeling.

One of the things about growing up which they're careful not to tell you is, you start having more things you don't talk to your parents about. And I had a doozie.

Hilda goes, "What's the matter, are you off Sugar Pops now? Honestly, Kelsey, I can't keep up with you! And why can't you wear something nicer than that old shirt to school? Oh, I get it: disguise, right?"

She sighed and looked at me kind of sad but smiling, her hands on her hips. "Kelsey, Kelsey," she goes, "if only I'd had half of what you've got when *I* was a girl—I was flat as an ironing board, and it made me so miserable, I can't tell you."

She's still real thin and neat-looking, so what does she know about it? But she meant well, and anyhow I was feeling so good I didn't argue.

I didn't change my shirt, though.

That night I didn't turn into a wolf. I laid there waiting, but though the moon came up, nothing happened no matter how hard I tried, and after a while I went and looked out the window and realized that the moon wasn't really full anymore, it was getting smaller.

I wasn't so much relieved as sorry. I bought a calendar at the school book sale two weeks later, and I checked the full moon nights coming up and waited anxiously to see what would happen.

Meantime, things rolled along as usual. I got a rash of zits on my chin. I would look in the mirror and think about my wolf-face, that had beautiful sleek fur instead of zits.

Zits and all I went to Angela Durkin's party, and next day Billy Linden told everybody that I went in one of the bedrooms at Angela's and made out with him, which I did not. But since no grown-ups were home and Fat Joey brought grass to the party, most of the kids were stoned and didn't know who did what or where anyhow.

As a matter of fact, Billy once actually did get a girl in Seven B high one time out in his parents' garage and him and two of his friends did it to her while she was zonked out of her mind, or anyway they said they did, and she was too embarrassed to say anything one way or the other, and a little while later she changed schools.

How I know about it is the same way everybody else does, which is because Billy was the biggest boaster in the whole school, and you could never tell if he was lying or not.

So I guess it wasn't so surprising that some people believed what Billy said about me. Gerry-Anne quit talking to me after that. Meantime Hilda got pregnant.

This turned into a huge discussion about how Hilda had been worried about her biological clock so she and Dad had decided to have a kid, and I shouldn't mind, it would be fun for me and good preparation for being a mother myself later on, when I found some nice guy and got married.

Sure. Great preparation. Like Mary O'Hare in my class, who gets to change her youngest baby sister's diapers all the time, yick. She jokes about it, but you can tell she really hates it. Now it looked like it was my turn coming up, as usual.

The only thing that made life bearable was my secret.

"You're laid back today," Devon Brown said to me in the lunchroom one day after Billy had been specially obnoxious, trying to flick rolled up pieces of bread from his table so they would land on my chest. Devon was sitting with me because he was bad at French, my only good subject, and I was helping him out with some verbs. I guess he wanted to know why I wasn't upset because of Billy picking on me. He goes, "How come?"

"That's a secret," I said, thinking about what Devon would say if he knew a werewolf was helping him with his French: *loup. Manger.*

He goes, "What secret?" Devon has freckles and is actually kind of cute-looking.

"A *secret*," I go, "so I can't tell you, dummy."

He looks real superior and he goes, "Well, it can't be much of a secret, because girls can't keep secrets, everybody knows that."

Sure, like that kid Sara in Eight B who it turned out her own father had been molesting her for years, but she never told anybody until some psychologist caught on from some tests we all had to take in seventh grade. Up till then, Sara kept her secret fine.

And I kept mine, marking off the days on the calendar. The only part I didn't look forward to was having a period again, which last time came right before the change.

When the time came, I got crampy and more zits popped out on my face, but I didn't have a period.

I changed, though.

The next morning they were talking in school about a couple of prize miniature schnauzers at the Wanscombes that had been hauled out of their yard by somebody and killed, and almost nothing left of them.

Well, my stomach turned a little when I heard some kids describing what Mr. Wanscombe had found over in Baker's Park, "the remains," as people said. I felt a little guilty, too, because Mrs. Wanscombe had really loved those little dogs, which somehow I didn't think about at all when I was a wolf the night before, trotting around hungry in the moonlight.

I knew those Schnauzers personally, so I was sorry, even if they were irritating little mutts that made a lot of noise.

But heck, the Wanscombes shouldn't have left them out all night in the cold. Anyhow, they were rich, they could buy new ones if they wanted.

Still and all, though. I mean, dogs are just dumb animals. If they're mean, it's because they're wired that way or somebody made them mean, they can't help it. They can't just decide to be nice, like a person can. And plus, they don't taste so great, I think because they put so much junk in commercial dog-foods—anti-worm medicine and ashes and ground up fish, stuff like that. Ick.

In fact after the second schnauzer I had felt sort of sick and I didn't sleep real well that night. So I was not in a great mood to start with; and that was the day that my new brassiere disappeared while I was in gym. Later on I got passed a note telling me where to find it: stapled to the bulletin board outside the Principal's office, where everybody could see that I was trying a bra with an underwire.

Naturally, it had to be Stacey Buhl that grabbed my bra while I was changing for gym and my back was turned, since she was now hanging out with Billy and his friends.

Billy went around all day making bets at the top of his lungs on how soon I would be wearing a D-cup.

Stacey didn't matter, she was just a jerk. Billy mattered.

He had wrecked me in that school forever, with his nasty mind and his big, fat mouth. I was past crying or fighting and getting punched out. I was boiling, I had had enough crap from him, and I had an idea.

I followed Billy home and waited on his porch until his mom came home and she made him come down and talk to me. He stood in the doorway and talked through the screen door, eating a banana and lounging around like he didn't have a care in the world.

So he goes, "Whatcha want, Boobs?"

I stammered a lot, being I was so nervous about telling such big lies, but that probably made me sound more believable.

I told him that I would make a deal with him: I would meet him that night in Baker's Park, late, and take off my shirt and bra and let him do whatever he wanted with my boobs if that would satisfy his curiosity and he would find somebody else to pick on and leave me alone.

"What?" he said, staring at my chest with his mouth open. His voice squeaked and he was practically drooling on the floor. He couldn't believe his good luck.

I said the same thing over again.

He almost came out onto the porch to try it right then and there. "Well, shit," he goes, lowering his voice a lot, "why didn't you say something before? You really mean it?"

I go, "Sure," though I couldn't look at him.

After a minute he goes, "Okay, it's a deal. Listen, Kelsey, if you like it, can we, uh, do it again, you know?"

I go, "Sure. But Billy, one thing: this is a secret, between just you and me. If you tell anybody, if there's one other person hanging around out there tonight—"

"Oh, no," he goes, real fast, "I won't say a thing to anybody, honest. Not a word, I promise!"

Not until afterward, of course, was what he meant, which if there was one thing Billy Linden couldn't do, it was to keep quiet if he knew something bad about another person.

"You're gonna like it, I know you are," he goes, speaking strictly for himself as usual. "Jeez. I can't believe this!"

But he did, the dork.

I couldn't eat much for dinner that night, I was too excited, and I went upstairs early to do homework, I told Dad and Hilda.

Then I waited for the moon, and when it came, I changed.

Billy was in the park. I caught a whiff of him, very sweaty and excited, but I stayed cool. I snuck around for a while, as quiet as I could—which was real quiet—making sure none of his stupid friends were lurking around. I mean, I wouldn't have trusted just his promise for a million dollars.

I passed up half a hamburger lying in the gutter where somebody had parked for lunch next to Baker's Park. My mouth watered, but I didn't want to spoil my appetite. I was hungry and happy, sort of singing inside my own head, "Shoo, fly, pie, and an apple-pan-dowdie . . ."

Without any sound, of course.

Billy had been sitting on a bench, his hands in his pockets, twisting around to look this way and that way, watching for me—for my human self—to come join him. He had a jacket on, being it was very chilly out.

Which he didn't stop to think that maybe a sane person wouldn't be crazy enough to sit out there and take off her top leaving her naked skin bare to the breeze. But that was Billy all right, totally fixed on his own greedy self and without a single thought for somebody else. I bet all he could think about was what a great scam this was, to feel up old Boobs in the park and then crow about it all over school.

Now he was walking around the park, kicking at the sprinkler-heads and glancing up every once in a while, frowning and looking sulky.

I could see he was starting to think that I might stand him up. Maybe he even suspected that old Boobs was lurking around watching him and laughing to herself because he had fallen for a trick. Maybe old Boobs had even brought some kids from school with her to see what a jerk he was.

Actually that would have been pretty good, except Billy probably would have broken my nose for me again, or worse, if I'd tried it.

"Kelsey?" he goes, sounding mad.

I didn't want him stomping off home in a huff. I moved up closer, and I let the bushes swish a little around my shoulders.

He goes, "Hey, Kelse, it's late, where've you been?"

I listened to the words, but mostly I listened to the little thread of worry flickering in his voice, low and high, high and low, as he tried to figure out what was going on.

I let out the whisper of a growl.

He stood real still, staring at the bushes, and he goes, "That you, Kelse? Answer me."

I was wild inside. I couldn't wait another second. I tore through the bushes and leaped for him, flying.

He stumbled backward with a squawk—"What!"—jerking his hands up in front of his face, and he was just sucking in a big breath to yell with when I hit him like a demo-derby truck.

I jammed my nose past his feeble claws and chomped down hard on his face.

No sound came out of him except this wet, thick gurgle, which I could more taste than hear because the sound came right into my mouth with the gush of his blood and the hot mess of meat and skin that I tore away and swallowed.

He thrashed around, hitting at me, but I hardly felt anything through my fur. I mean, he wasn't so big and strong laying there on the ground with me straddling him all lean and wiry with wolf-muscle. And plus, he was in shock. I got a strong whiff from below as he let go of everything right into his pants.

Dogs were barking, but so many people around Baker's Park have dogs to keep out burglars, and the dogs make such a racket all the time, that nobody pays any attention. I wasn't worried. Anyway, I was too busy to care.

I nosed in under what was left of Billy's jaw and I bit his throat out.

Now let him go around telling lies about people.

His clothes were a lot of trouble and I really missed having hands. I managed to drag his shirt out of his belt with my teeth, though, and it was easy to tear his belly open. Pretty messy, but once I got in there, it was better

than Thanksgiving dinner. Who would think that somebody as horrible as Billy Linden could taste so *good?*

He was barely moving by then, and I quit thinking
about him as Billy Linden anymore. I quit thinking at
all, I just pushed my head in and pulled out delicious
steaming chunks and ate until I was picking at tidbits,
and everything was getting cold.

On the way home I saw a police car cruising the
neighborhood the way they do sometimes. I hid in the
shadows and of course they never saw me.

There was a lot of washing up to do in the morning,
and when Hilda saw my sheets she shook her head and
she goes, "You should be more careful about keeping
track of your period so as not to get caught by surprise."

Everybody in school knew something had happened to Billy Linden, but it wasn't until the day after
that they got the word. Kids stood around in little hud-
dles trading rumors about how some wild animal had
chewed Billy up. I would walk up and listen in and add a
really gross remark or two, like part of the game of
thrilling each other green and nauseous with made-up
details to see who would upchuck first.

Not me, that's for sure. I mean, when somebody
went on about how Billy's whole head was gnawed down
to the skull and they didn't even know who he was except
from the bus pass in his wallet, I got a little urpy. It's amazing the things people will dream up. But when I thought
about what I had actually done to Billy, I had to smile.

It felt totally wonderful to walk through the halls
without having anybody yelling, "Hey, Boobs!"

Even my social life is looking up. Gerry-Anne is not
only talking to me again, she invited me out on a
double-date with her. Some guy she met at a party asked

her to go to the movies with him next weekend, and he has a friend. They're both from Fawcett Junior High across town, which will be a change. I was nervous when she asked me, but finally I said yes. My first real date!

I am still pretty nervous, to tell the truth. I have to keep promising myself that I will not worry about my chest, I will not be self-conscious, even if the guy stares.

Actually things at school are not completely hunky-dory. Hilda says, "That's Life" when I complain about things, and I am beginning to believe her. Fat Joey somehow got to be my lab-partner in Science, and if he doesn't quit trying to grab a feel whenever we have to stand close together to do an experiment, he is going to be sorry.

He doesn't know it, but he's got until the next full moon.

SPECTERS IN THE MOONLIGHT

Larry Segriff

Plese, Daddy. Please don't."

The soft little voice cut across my dreams, jerking me awake. There was that moment of disorientation that always accompanies waking up in a strange room, especially in the middle of the night.

I looked over at the pillow next to mine, knowing damn well there was no one there. But that voice had been so real, that note of quiet desperation so heart wrenching, that I just had to look.

The pillow was empty except for the wan, pale moonlight shining through the frost on the window and the little lace curtains. It lit up my room, and touched my heart with its chill. For a moment it lay there, black and silver on the pillowcase, and then a cloud swept across it and took it away.

A cold night in the middle of nowhere. This little bed and breakfast had been recommended to me—so much so that I stopped a hundred miles short of my destination to stay here, and that with a big presentation in the morning.

I glanced at the clock beside the bed. 2:30. Only three hours before I had to get up, and I needed my sleep. I'd been a sales rep for the same pharmaceutical company for a long time, and it seemed that these days I had to work harder than ever just to keep up. Opportunities like this one were fewer and farther between than they once were. I couldn't afford to blow it.

Rolling over, I plumped the pillow beneath me, pulled the quilt up over my shoulders again, and settled down once more.

"Please, Daddy, please not again."

"Damn!" I said, flinging the covers back and sitting up in bed before I even knew what I was doing. Automatically, I glanced once at the little sample case I kept on the floor by my bed, but then I looked away. There was nothing in there that would help this.

Not yet, anyway.

Feeling the beginnings of anger stirring within me, I got out of bed and, not even bothering to fumble for my slippers, stalked around to the other side. That voice had sounded like it was right next to my head. There had to be a speaker in the pillow or the headboard or something. Presentation or no, I was going to find it, and then I was going to raise some holy hell.

Grimly, I set about stripping the bed.

I found nothing. The bed was an old four-poster. Oak, I thought, but in the cloudshot moonlight it was hard to tell. I searched it as carefully as I could for about fifteen minutes, and came away completely empty. No hidden compartments in the wood. No lumps in the pillow or the mattress. No hollow sounds in the wall behind the bed.

Nothing. Not a damned thing.

Frowning, my mind racing as it examined options and possibilities, my hands went through the unthinking process of making the bed up again. Not that I was necessarily planning on returning to it—I hadn't decided about that yet—but out of old habit. One of the first lessons I learned was to leave things as I found them. There weren't many bridges in this business; it wasn't safe to burn any of them.

I had just finished replacing the pillows and had stepped back from the bed to survey my handiwork when I heard the voice again. This time it was just a single word, "Please," softer and more drawn out than before, and the pain in it was enough to break my heart and drain away the anger building within me.

But that wasn't what chilled me to my very soul, nor was it the faint sobbing that followed on its heels. No, what froze me in place was the fact that the moon had come out once again, and from this vantage point I could see the pattern it made as it passed through the lace on its way to the pillow.

That pattern was a face.

Oh, not like Rembrandt might have painted—the eyes were too big, and the mouth too wide, and the nose more of a suggestion than an actual representation—but

it didn't take much imagination to see it as a face. And
the longer I looked, the more lifelike it became.

Had there been moonlight that second time I
heard the voice? I couldn't recall. I'd been angry, and
not paying attention to such things.

I shook my head. What was I doing? Was I really
starting to think—?

Again a cloud passed before the moon and the sobbing cut off.

My God, I thought, sinking slowly down on the edge
of the bed. *What's going on?* This was . . . this was mad-
ness. Such things simply didn't happen.

I leaned back and felt the solidity of my sample case.
This was reality. Not specters in the moonlight, but *this*.

But that voice, that pain . . .

I don't know how long I sat there, or what decision
I might have reached on my own, because eventually
the moon came out again and all choices were taken
from me.

This time, the moon lay full upon the bed, and in
the patterns of shadows I could see more than just a face.
I could see a full person. There were the shoulders, and
there the arms, raised in futile defense. There were the
legs, spread shamelessly, and the back arched in pain.

"Oh, sweet Jesus," I whispered as her sobs once more
filled the room. "How can I stop this? What can I do?"

But there were no answers among the shadows and
the sobs. Just the silver moonlight, and the sounds of
suffering.

"Daddy . . ." That single word hung on the night air,
a loud cry that came as a plea and an accusation, and
pierced me with its pain.

I knew then that I was going to do something foolish. The second rule of business is Don't Get Involved. Well, that rule had just shattered along with my heart.

I was involved, whether I wanted to be or not.

Pulled to my feet by the pain in that voice, I stumbled over to my sample case. There was a gun concealed in a side pocket. When I'd first started out in this business, such a thing was unthinkable. Now it was mandatory.

I wanted that gun. With it, I might be able to force some answers from someone. Besides, I needed to feel its comfortable, deadly weight in my hand.

Pulling it out, I turned back to the shadowy form on my bed.

"I'll be back," I promised her. She didn't react at all, didn't acknowledge me in any way, but I felt certain she'd heard me—heard me and understood the promise I was making.

Then, the sound of her sobbing still echoing in my head, I went out to find the man who'd put them there.

He was in the living room on the floor below, waiting for me. He was sitting in a rocking chair, an afghan across his old, withered knees, his chair turned slightly toward the picture window. His silhouette was black against the moonlight.

Beside him, on the floor, I could see his wooden cane. He'd used it when he'd met me at the door, and when he'd shown me up to my room. It was all a single piece of wood—rosewood, I'd guessed, and its handle had been carved into the shape of a rose. Exquisitely wrought, I'd thought it a wonderful thing to own, its beauty almost worth the pain its use must cost him.

Now it just lay there like a guilty burden he'd tried to cast aside.

I thought he was asleep, but his head lifted as I came down the stairs. As I drew closer, I could see that he held something in his lap. It glinted briefly and for a moment my finger tightened on the trigger, but it wasn't a weapon. It was a picture, an old framed photograph of a young girl, and any doubts I may have had fled at the sight.

"Damned weathermen," he said as I came up beside him. He gestured toward the window with the small photograph in his hand. "Said it was supposed to be cloudy all night. Wouldn't have put you in that room otherwise. Wouldn't have put you there anyway except we're all full up. No choice."

But I didn't want to hear that. I was surprised to note that my hand had grown sweaty on the grip of the pistol I held. That was unlike me, but then this whole situation was unlike me.

"Tell me," I said. "Tell me about her."

He looked once at the gun in my hand. "You can put that away," he said. I didn't, and after a moment he sighed and looked down again at the picture in his hand. "Her name was Rose. She was my daughter. When she was fourteen, she took a whole bottle of sleeping pills—they'd been her mother's; I guess I'd never gotten around to throwing them out after Lydia died. Rose died in her bed. It was late October, and there was a Harvest Moon that night, shining down full and bright. I like to think its light showed her the way home."

My hand had started to cramp around the grip of my pistol and I flexed my fingers once to keep them loose. "Go on," I said.

"Not much more to say," he said. Reaching down, he fumbled around and came up with his cane. Reflexively, I took a step back, and kept my gun leveled at his chest. "I carved this out of the same wood I made her cross from. You can still see it. She's buried in the cemetery at the top of the hill, just down the road a ways."

He sighed again, and sort of slumped deeper into his chair before lapsing back into silence.

I flexed my fingers a second time. Listening to him speak, I'd felt my anger lessen a bit, but now it was back. "That's it? That's all you have to say? No apologies? No excuses?"

"Son," he said, and this time there was a hint of fire in his voice, "I made my apologies years ago. I don't see any call to repeat them to you. Besides, that's not what you're after. You're here to lay that ghost to rest, and you know I'm the only one who can do that, so put that gun away and let's get on with it."

I frowned, and flexed my fingers a third time, but neither seemed to help. The truth was, he was right. "How?" I said, hating the fact that I had to ask.

"Simple. I have to die as she did. It's the only thing that will give her peace. It's got to be in that bed, and it has to be an overdose of drugs—which is why I keep telling you to put that gun away. You don't need it, and you can't help her with it. Oh, and one other thing: it's got to be a night like this, with the full moon shining down."

"How do you know all this?"

"I asked, is how. Son, I've been trying to end her suffering for nigh on thirty years. I've had the priest out.

The old coot won't admit she's real, but he says that even if she was, there'd be nothing he could do. Demons, yes, he's got rituals for them, but not for ghosts. So I've had others out, over the years, people who do this for a living. They all told me that I was the only one who could help her. I wasn't ready, then; still had some living to do, but that's all behind me now. I'm an old man, and I don't want to meet my maker with her spirit still lost in this world."

If he was trying to play on my sympathies, it wasn't working. The echoes of her pain were still too loud in my memory. They drowned out any feelings I might have for him.

"So why haven't you done it?" I asked. "If it's that simple, why haven't you done it yourself?"

He shook his head in the moonlight. "I couldn't do that. The Bible says suicide's a sin. I told you, I don't want to meet my maker with her spirit still lost, and that's the truth, but even less do I want to stand before Saint Peter and tell him I killed myself. No, sir. Rose is my daughter, and I want her to find peace, but I don't want to spend eternity in hell for her."

Listening to his words, I decided that I didn't believe him. I didn't want to, for one thing. I'd seen too much pain and suffering up in that room to want to believe he was truly sorry.

But it was more than that. Mostly, it was that his story was just too pat, too slick. I was a salesman myself. I recognized a pitch when I heard one.

The trick was going to be separating out the truth in what he'd just said. From my own experience, I knew that the best way to hook a customer was through honesty. Tell 'em enough to give your line that ring of sincerity, and then lead them astray. I was pretty sure that was what he was trying on me.

The question was, which parts were true?

I didn't have to think about that for long. The answer became obvious as soon as I turned it around: which part was false? Clearly, I realized, the part about his wanting to die was a lie. I didn't believe it. I refused to believe it. Which meant that the other part, the bit about how his daughter could be helped, that was probably true.

"All right," I said. "I'll help you." And I would, too. Only not the way he had it planned. "You lead the way," I added, stepping back out of reach.

He didn't protest, just struggled up out of his chair and started up the stairs.

At the top of the stairs, he paused. "Pills are in there," he said, using his cane to point toward the bathroom at the end of the hall, "but you'll have to feed them to me. I don't want to do anything that'll make it look like I'm helping you."

And suddenly I saw it all. Of course. It was the pills. Sure, he'd known this would happen someday, that sooner or later someone would meet poor Rose, and come to him for some answers. He must have made up a whole bottle of fakes—probably just ordinary sugar spooned into regular gel caps. All he'd have to do is swallow a bunch of them, go to sleep, and that would be that. By the time I knew he was still alive, the other guests would be awake. Even more importantly, the moon would be gone from the sky, and it would be too late.

That was his plan. I knew it. It had to be. Only it wasn't going to work quite that way.

"All right," I said. "I'll get them in a moment."

He paused outside my room, and I could see his shoulders stiffen beneath the thin robe he wore. Carefully, I reached around him and turned the knob. "After you," I said, and pushed the door open.

She was still there. She was lying on her side, her tear-tracked face turned toward the window, and silent sobs racked her shadowy form.

"Rose." It was the old man who spoke. He took a single step into the room, his free hand reaching out toward the bed.

"Let's go," I said. I stepped up beside him and in one move took his cane away from him and propelled him onto the bed. At that point, I didn't give a damn about his frail old bones.

"The pills . . ." he said, but I ignored him and made my way back to my sample case.

I didn't spend any time thinking about what I was about to do. I could see her lying there beside him, her soft sobs as regular as a heartbeat, and I felt no remorse at all as I spun the locks. A moment later and my case was open, with all my goodies laid out in their neat little rows.

I glanced up at the old man, to make sure he wasn't watching me. I kept my hands below the level of the lid, to block his sight, but I didn't want to take any chances. After all, even though he was pretty much a helpless old man and couldn't stop me if he tried, still I didn't want him waking up any of the other guests.

I saw right away that I didn't have to worry. He was enrapt by the ghost at his side. He had one hand on her shoulder, and though I imagined he was trying to apologize, it looked for all the world like he was caressing her. I nodded once and started thumbing through my supplies.

Soon I had it, a syringe full of liquid death, shining silver in the moonlight.

I looked at them, once, father and daughter, and then I made my move, stepping forward, bringing up my hand, plunging the needle deep into his backside, and driving the plunger home.

He jerked, but by then it was too late. I withdrew the needle and stepped back, ready for almost anything. Anything, that is, except what happened.

He looked at me, looked at the needle in my hand, and smiled.

"Thank you," he said.

I took another step back, this time in confusion. Had I misunderstood? Was he truly repentant?

I got no farther in my thoughts. The stuff I gave him was fast acting, and I saw him slump forward, his left arm flying out and passing through his daughter.

"Rose," he whispered, "I'm coming, Rose."

And there in the moonlight I saw her turn toward him. I saw her eyes go wide, and her mouth stretch in a scream that was beyond my power to hear. And then I saw him rise up out of his body and wrap her in a vile, loving embrace.

I staggered back in horror, looking at what I had wrought. With my mind's eye, I could see the scene before me stretching out for all of eternity. I could hear her screams in my head, her cries of utter anguish, and I knew that I had caused them.

I looked at the two of them and the scene before me burned its way into my heart. I knew in that moment that I couldn't let this go on. I had to stop it, and I thought I knew how.

My hand brushed my sample case as I tossed the useless gun onto the bed. I glanced down into it, and started rummaging through its contents again.

Moments later, I lay down on the bed next to the old man, the rosewood cane gripped firmly in my left hand. On the other side of him, the two spirits writhed, one in pleasure, one in agony.

I thought once, briefly, about my family, about what this would do to them, about what people would think, and then I put them out of my mind forever. There was simply no choice.

For the last time, I looked over at Rose, trying to blot her father from my vision, and then I said the very words he'd said to her.

"I'm coming, Rose," I said.

The silver moonlight lay full upon us as I emptied the needle into my arm and waited for it to show me the way to her side.

THERE'S NO SUCH THING

Charles de Lint

"Ken Parry," Apples said.

Cassie nodded.

"Is a vampire."

Cassie nodded again.

Apples had heard that Ken needled the kids he baby-sat, but this was the first she'd heard about his claiming to be a vampire.

"But there's no such thing," she said.

"Samantha said she saw him turn into a bat one night—right in front of her house when he didn't think she was looking. He was baby-sitting her, and instead of walking home when her parents got back, he *flew*."

"Flew?"

Cassie nodded solemnly.

Apples tapped her hairbrush against her hand, then set it down on her dresser.

Their mother had been heavily into mythology when she got out of the university, which was how, though they had a nice normal surname like Smith, the two girls got saddled with their given names of Appoline and Cassandra. Apples had looked them both up at the public library one day, hoping to find something she could use to stop the incessant teasing that they got, but Appoline just meant having something to do with Apollo—the Greek god of music, poetry, archery, prophecy, and healing. That sounded nice on paper, but came out sucky when you tried to explain it to someone. Cassandra had been a prophetess who Apollo was all hot and heavy over—and that would really be fuel for some bad-news ribbing if it ever got out.

Apples wasn't much good with music or poetry. She was lucky to get a C in either at school. She couldn't read the future, and about the most she could do along the healing line was put on a Band-Aid. But hunting milkweed seedpods in the field behind her house as a kid, she'd learned to shoot a mean arrow. Trouble was, that didn't mean much when you were sixteen—not unless you were planning to go in for the Olympics or something, which wasn't exactly an ambition that Apples had set her sights upon.

Cassie couldn't read the future either. She was a sweet eight-year-old with curly blond hair and a smile that just wouldn't quit. She should have had a great life laid out in front of her, except she had severe asthma so she couldn't go anywhere without her bronchodilator. Then there was her right leg, which was half the size of her left and a good three inches shorter. The only way she could walk around was by wearing a leg brace that gained her sympathy, or weird stares, but wasn't exactly endearing.

Except to Apples. She'd do anything for Cassie.

But give up her first date with Rob D'Lima, considering that she'd been mooning over him for three months before he finally asked her out?

"You know there's really no such thing as vampires," she said.

Cassie only regarded her with all the gravity that an eight-year-old can muster when they know they're right but can't prove it.

Apples sighed.

"I've seen him in the middle of the day," she said. "I thought they couldn't go out in the sunlight."

"That's just part of their legend," Cassie explained. "They've made up all kinds of things about themselves so that people will think they're safe from them. You know, like the bit with the mirror . . . and crosses and garlic. The only thing that's real is that they have to be invited into your house, and Mom and Dad have *done* that."

Apples picked up her hairbrush again.

"You're really scared, aren't you?" she said.

"Wouldn't you be?"

Apples smiled. "I guess I would. Okay. I'll stay home with you tonight."

"It won't do any good."

Apples thought Cassie was talking about her date with Rob.

"If Rob's half as nice as I think he is, he'll understand," she said. "Maybe he'll even come over, and the three of us can . . ."

Her voice trailed off as Cassie started shaking her head.

"I already asked Mom," Cassie said, "and she said no way."

"You told her Ken was a vampire?"

"I had to . . ."

Apples sighed again. While Cassie hadn't been gifted with the ability to see into the future, she *had* been born with an overactive imagination. Their parents had long since lost patience with her stories.

"You should have come to me first," Apples said.

"You were late coming back from volleyball practice, and I didn't know if you'd be back in time for me to tell you about it."

"I'm sorry."

"It's okay."

"So what can we do about this?" Apples asked.

"Could you, maybe, come home early . . . ?"

Apples smiled and tousled her sister's hair. "You bet. I'll be back as soon as the movie's over. We'll send Ken packing, and then we'll pig out on popcorn and watch some music videos."

"It'll be past my bedtime."

Apples laughed. "Like that's ever stopped you."

ROB WAS REALLY NICE about it. After the show was over, they went back to Apples's house. Ken seemed surprised to see them, but that was about it. No fangs. No big black cape. Apples paid him from the house money her mom kept in a jar in the pantry cupboard and closed the front door behind him.

"Just let me go check on the Munchkin," Apples said as Rob settled down on the couch. "Won't take a moment. You . . ." She hesitated. "If she wants to sit up with us for a little while, you won't mind, will you?"

Rob shook his head. "That's one of the things I like about you, Apples: the way you take care of Cassie. Most kids hate their little brothers and sisters. Me, I just wish I had one."

"Well you can share mine tonight," Apples said.

"I'll hold you to that."

Be still, my heart, Apples thought as she headed upstairs to Cassie's room.

She was thinking about how it would feel to have Rob kiss her when she stepped into the room and her heartbeat jumped into double time. Cassie was huddled on her bed, hunched over and making wheezing sounds.

Oh, jeez, Apples thought, she's having an attack and that bloody fool Ken never checked on her.

But when she got to Cassie's bed, she found that her sister was crying, not struggling for breath. Apples sat down on the bed, the bedsprings dipping under her weight. Before she could reach out a hand, Cassie had turned and buried her face against Apples's shoulder.

"It's okay, it's okay," Apples murmured, stroking Cassie's short hair.

She was going to kill Ken Parry.

"What happened?" she asked.

"He . . . he . . ."

Apples had an awful thought.

"Did he . . . touch you, Cassie?"

Cassie nodded and started to sob louder. Apples held her until her crying had subsided; then she brushed the damp hair away from Cassie's brow and had a good look at her little sister. There were questions she knew she should ask, but somehow she felt the best thing to do right now was to get Cassie over the immediate trauma. The poor kid looked miserable. Her face was all puffed up and her eyes were red. She sniveled, then blew her nose when Apples handed her a tissue.

"He said," Cassie began. She hesitated, then started over. "I . . . I woke up and he . . . he was sitting on the bed and he'd pulled my nightie up, but then . . . then you came home . . ."

"Oh, Cassie."

"He . . . he said if I told anyone, he'd come back in the night and he'd . . . he'd hurt me . . ."

"No one's going to come and no one's going to hurt you," Apples told her. "I promise you."

"Everything all right in here?"

Apples looked up to find Rob standing in the doorway. She nodded.

"Ken just scared her, that's all," she said.

She felt inordinately pleased when she saw his hands clench into fists at his sides and anger flare up in his eyes.

"Sounds like this guy needs a lesson in—"

Apples cut him off.

"There's not much we can do—not without getting into trouble ourselves. This is the kind of thing my parents are going to have to handle."

"But . . ."

Apples gave a meaningful nod to her sister—it said, Not in front of Cassie, please—and was grateful to see that he caught its meaning without her having to actually say the words aloud.

He took a breath, then let it out slowly and put a smile on his face.

"You promised me some popcorn," he said. "I hope you're not going back on the deal now."

Apples gave him a grateful look. "Not a chance. How about you, Cassie? Do you feel like having some with us, or are you going to make us eat it all on our own? You know me, I eat like a bird. Maybe I should put mine in a bird feeder."

The smile she got back was small, but it was there, and by the time the popcorn was popping in the microwave and a Richard Marx video was booming from the television set, Cassie was almost back to her old self again. All except for the hurt look in the back of her eyes that Apples was afraid might never go away.

ROB LEFT BEFORE HER parents got back.

"You're going to talk to them about this guy?" he asked when they were standing out on the stoop.

"I'll get it all worked out," Apples said. "I promise."

"But if you need some help . . ."

"You'll be the first I'll call."

The kiss was everything she'd hoped it would be— multiplied maybe a hundred times more. She felt a little breathless as she watched him go down the walk, and the tingle he'd called up from deep inside her didn't go away for hours.

She was in bed when her parents got home and didn't say anything to them except for a sleepy good night that was half muffled by her pillow. She waited until she was sure they were asleep before she got up again.

She couldn't get Ken Parry out of her mind. Not even thinking of Rob helped. Her mind just kept coming back to Ken and what he'd tried to do to Cassie.

Mr. Vampire. Right.

She had to talk to him, and talk to him now. But first she had to get his attention. With a guy like Ken, there was only one way to do that.

She went to her closet and rummaged around in it until she came up with a black leather miniskirt and a scoop-necked blouse. She brushed her hair and tied it back, put on a slash of red lipstick, then tiptoed down the stairs and out of the house. She put her high heels on when she was outside and click-clacked her way along the sidewalk, two blocks north, one block west, another north, until she was standing in front of Ken Parry's house.

The streetlight cast enough light for her to make out the Batman poster in the left front bedroom on the second floor. There was only one kid living here, so it had to be his room.

Stooping awkwardly in the short skirt, she picked up some small bits of gravel from the Parry driveway and tossed them up at the window. It took three tries before a very sleepy-looking Ken Parry slid up the window and peered down at her.

He woke up quickly when he saw who it was.

"What do you want?" he called down in a loud whisper.

"I thought we could make a trade," she whispered back. "I'll give you something you'll like and you leave my little sister alone."

"You're kidding."

Apples put a hand on her waist and thrust out a hip. "Do I look like I'm kidding?"

He made a soft noise in the back of his throat.

"I . . . I'll be right down."

When he opened the door, she was standing on the porch.

"Aren't you going to invite me in?" she purred.

"I . . . my parents . . ."

"Are sleeping, I'll bet."

"Uh, sure. You, uh, come on in."

He stood aside to let her pass by.

Apples gave him a considering look as she stepped into his house—just to be sure. One look at him was all it took to confirm it. Ken Parry wasn't a vampire. She should know. Her only regret as she let him lead her downstairs to the rec room was that his dumb stunt had forced her to tell Cassie:

There's no such thing as vampires.

Because it was the first time she'd ever lied to her little sister.

KEN PARRY NEVER CAME back to school. Rumor in the halls had it that he'd come down with a kind of anemia that the doctors simply couldn't diagnose. It left him too weak for normal teenage pursuits; so weak that he ended up staying in the hospital until his family finally moved away just before midterm exams.

Apples didn't miss him. She only needed to feed once a month, and there were always other people around, just like him, who got their kicks out of tormenting some little kid.

She didn't give Ken or any of them the Gift itself—not the way that the woman had given her the Gift in the parking lot behind the Civic Center after a Bryan Adams concert this past summer. She never did find out why the woman chose her. All she knew was that vampires lived forever, and she didn't want any of those guys around for that long.

No, she was saving the Gift. Vampires never got sick, and if there was something wrong with them when they got that special bite, then the Gift cured them. So she was waiting for Cassie to turn sixteen.

Until then she had to figure out a way to deal with her parents' always remarking on how she just never seemed to get any older. And she had to decide if Rob really was someone she'd want to be with forever.

Because forever took on a whole different meaning for those with the Gift.

THE CHILD THAT WENT WITH THE FAIRIES

J. Sheridan Le Fanu

Eastward of the old city of Limerick, about ten Irish miles under the range of mountains known as the Slieveelim hills, famous as having afforded Sarsfield a shelter among their rocks and hollows, when he crossed them in his gallant descent upon the cannon and ammunition of King William, on its way to the beleaguering army, there runs a very old and narrow road. It connects the Limerick road to Tipperary with the old road from Limerick to Dublin, and runs by bog and pasture, hill and hollow, straw-thatched village, and roofless castle, not far from twenty miles.

Skirting the healthy mountains of which I have spoken, at one part it becomes singularly lonely. For more than three Irish miles it traverses a deserted country. A wide, black bog, level as a lake, skirted with copse, spreads at the left, as you journey northward, and the long and irregular line of mountain rises at the right, clothed in heath, broken with lines of grey rock that resemble the bold and irregular outlines of fortifications, and riven with many a gully, expanding here and there into rocky and wooded glens, which open as they approach the road.

A scanty pasturage, on which browsed a few scattered sheep or kine, skirts this solitary road for some miles, and under shelter of a hillock, and of two or three great ash-trees, stood, not many years ago, the little thatched cabin of a widow named Mary Ryan.

Poor was this widow in a land of poverty. The thatch had acquired the grey tint and sunken outlines, that show how the alternations of rain and sun have told upon that perishable shelter.

But whatever other dangers threatened, there was one well provided against by the care of other times. Round the cabin stood half a dozen mountain ashes, as the rowans, inimical to witches, are there called. On the worn planks of the door were nailed two horseshoes, and over the lintel and spreading along the thatch, grew, luxuriant, patches of that ancient cure for many maladies, and prophylactic against the machinations of the evil one, the house-leek. Descending into the doorway, in the *chiaroscuro* of the interior, when your eye grew sufficiently accustomed to that dim light, you might discover, hanging at the head of the widow's wooden-roofed bed, her beads and a phial of holy water.

Here certainly were defences and bulwarks against the intrusion of that unearthly and evil power, of whose vicinity this solitary family were constantly reminded by the outline of Lisnavoura, that lonely hill-haunt of the "Good people," as the fairies are called euphemistically, whose strangely dome-like summit rose not half a mile away, looking like an outwork of the long line of mountain that sweeps by it.

It was at the fall of the leaf, and an autumnal sunset threw the lengthening shadow of haunted Lisnavoura, close in front of the solitary little cabin, over the undulating slopes and sides of Slieveelim. The birds were singing among the branches in the thinning leaves of the melancholy ash-trees that grew at the roadside in front of the door. The widow's three younger children were playing on the road, and their voices mingled with the evening song of the birds. Their elder sister, Nell, was "within in the house," as their phrase is, seeing after the boiling of the potatoes for supper.

Their mother had gone down to the bog, to carry up a hamper of turf on her back. It is, or was at least, a charitable custom—and if not disused, long may it continue—for the wealthier people when cutting their turf and stacking it in the bog, to make a smaller stack for the behoof of the poor, who were welcome to take from it so long as it lasted, and thus the potato pot was kept boiling, and hearth warm that would have been cold enough but for that good-natured bounty, through wintry months.

Moll Ryan trudged up the steep "bohereen" whose banks were overgrown with thorn and brambles, and stooping under her burden, re-entered her door, where her dark-haired daughter Nell met her with a welcome, and relieved her of her hamper.

Moll Ryan looked round with a sigh of relief, and drying her forehead, uttered the Munster ejaculation:

"Eiah, wisha! It's tired I am with it, God bless it. And where's the craythurs, Nell?"

"Playin' out on the road, mother; didn't ye see them and you comin' up?"

"No; there was no one before me on the road," she said, uneasily; "not a soul, Nell; and why didn't ye keep an eye on them?"

"Well, they're in the haggard, playin' there, or round by the back o' the house. Will I call them in?"

"Do so, good girl, in the name o' God. The hens is comin' home see, and the sun was just down over Knockdoulah, an' I comin' up."

So out ran tall, dark-haired Nell, and standing on the road, looked up and down it; but not a sign of her two little brothers, Con and Bill, or her little sister, Peg, could she see. She called them; but no answer came from the little haggard, fenced with straggling bushes. She listened, but the sound of their voices was missing. Over the stile, and behind the house she ran—but there all was silent and deserted.

She looked down toward the bog, as far as she could see; but they did not appear. Again she listened— but in vain. At first she had felt angry, but now a different feeling overcame her, and she grew pale. With an undefined boding she looked toward the heathy boss of Lisnavoura, now darkening into the deepest purple against the flaming sky of sunset.

Again she listened with a sinking heart, and heard nothing but the farewell twitter and whistle of the birds in the bushes around. How many stories had she listened to by the winter hearth, of children stolen by the fairies, at nightfall, in lonely places! With this fear she knew her mother was haunted.

No one in the country round gathered her little flock about her so early as this frightened widow, and no door "in the seven parishes" was barred so early.

Sufficiently fearful, as all young people in that part of the world are of such dreaded and subtle agents, Nell was even more than usually afraid of them, for her terrors were infected and redoubled by her mother's. She was looking towards Lisnavoura in a trance of fear, and crossed herself again and again, and whispered prayer after prayer. She was interrupted by her mother's voice on the road calling her loudly. She answered, and ran round to the front of the cabin, where she found her standing.

"And where in the world's the craythurs—did ye see sight o' them anywhere?" cried Mrs. Ryan, as the girl came over the stile.

"Arrah! mother, 'tis only what they're run down the road a bit. We'll see them this minute coming back. It's like goats they are, climbin' here and runnin' there; an' if I had them here, in my hand, maybe I wouldn't give them a hiding all round."

"May the Lord forgive you, Nell! the childhers gone. They're took, and not a soul near us, and Father Tom three miles away! And what'll I do, or who's to help us this night? Oh, wirristhru, wirristhru! The craythurs is gone!"

"Whisht, mother, be aisy: don't ye see them comin' up?"

And then she shouted in menacing accents, waving her arm, and beckoning the children, who were seen approaching on the road, which some little way off made a slight dip, which had concealed them. They were approaching from the westward, and from the direction of the dreaded hill of Lisnavoura.

But there were only two of the children, and one of them, the little girl, was crying. Their mother and sister hurried forward to meet them, more alarmed than ever.

"Where is Billy—where is he?" cried the mother, nearly breathless, so soon as she was within hearing.

"He's gone—they took him away; but they said he'll come back again," answered little Con, with the dark brown hair.

"He's gone away with the grand ladies," blubbered the little girl.

"What ladies—where? Oh, Leum, asthora! My darlin', are you gone away at last? Where is he? Who took him? What ladies are you talkin' about? What way did he go?" she cried in distraction.

"I couldn't see where he went, mother; 'twas like as if he was going to Lisnavoura."

With a wild exclamation the distracted woman ran on towards the hill alone, clapping her hands, and crying aloud the name of her lost child.

Scared and horrified, Nell, not daring to follow, gazed after her, and burst into tears; and the other children raised high their lamentations in shrill rivalry.

Twilight was deepening. It was long past the time when they were usually barred securely within their habitation. Nell led the younger children into the cabin, and made them sit down by the turf fire, while she stood in the open door, watching in great fear for the return of her mother.

After a long while they did see their mother return. She came in and sat down by the fire, and cried as if her heart would break.

"Will I bar the doore, mother?" asked Nell.

"Ay, do—didn't I lose enough, this night, without lavin' the doore open, for more o' yez to go; but first take an' sprinkle a dust o' the holy waters over ye, acuishla, and bring it here till I throw a taste iv it over myself and the craythurs; an' I wondher, Nell, you'd forget to do the like yourself, lettin' the craythurs out so near nightfall. Come here and sit on my knees, asthora, come to me, mavourneen, and hould me fast, in the name o' God, and I'll hould you fast that none can take yez from me, and tell me all about it, and what it was—the Lord between us and harm—an' how it happened, and who was in it."

And the door being barred, the two children, some-times speaking together, often interrupting one another, often interrupted by their mother, managed to tell this strange story, which I had better relate connectedly and in my own language.

The Widow Ryan's three children were playing, as I have said, upon the narrow old road in front of her door. Little Bill or Leum, about five years old, with golden hair and large blue eyes, was a very pretty boy, with all the clear tints of healthy childhood, and that gaze of earnest simplicity which belongs not to town children of the same age. His little sister Peg, about a year older, and his brother Con, a little more than a year elder than she, made up the little group.

Under the great old ash-trees, whose last leaves were falling at their feet, in the light of an October sunset, they were playing with the hilarity and eagerness of rustic children, clamouring together, and their faces were turned toward the west and storied hill of Lisnavoura.

Suddenly a startling voice with a screech called to them from behind, ordering them to get out of the way, and turning, they saw a sight, such as they never beheld before. It was a carriage drawn by four horses that were pawing and snorting, in impatience, as if just pulled up. The children were almost under their feet, and scrambled to the side of the road next their own door.

This carriage and all its appointments were old-fashioned and gorgeous, and presented to the children, who had never seen anything finer than a turf car, and once, an old chaise that passed that way from Killaloe, a spectacle perfectly dazzling.

Here was antique splendour. The harness and trappings were scarlet, and blazing with gold. The horses were huge, and snow white, with great manes, that as they tossed and shook them in the air, seemed to stream and float sometimes longer and sometimes shorter, like so much smoke—their tails were long, and tied up in bows of broad scarlet and gold ribbon. The coach itself was glowing with colours, gilded and emblazoned. There were footmen in gay liveries, and three-cocked hats, like the coachman's; but he had a great wig, like a Judge's, and their hair was frizzed out and powdered, and a long thick "pigtail," with a bow to it, hung down the back of each.

All these servants were diminutive, and ludicrously out of proportion with the enormous horses of the equipage, and had sharp, sallow features, and small, restless fiery eyes, and faces of cunning and malice that chilled the children. The little coachman was scowling and showing his white fangs under his cocked hat, and his little blazing beads of eyes were quivering with fury in their sockets as he whirled his whip round and round over their heads, till the lash of it looked like a streak of fire in the evening sun, and sounded like the cry of a legion of "fillapoueeks" in the air.

"Stop the princess on the highway!" cried the coachman, in a piercing treble.

"Stop the princess on the highway!" piped each footman in turn, scowling over his shoulder down on the children and grinding his keen teeth.

The children were so frightened they could only gape and turn white in their panic. But a very sweet voice from the open window of the carriage reassured them, and arrested the attack of the lackeys.

A beautiful and "very grand-looking" lady was smiling from it on them, and they all felt pleased in the strange light of that smile.

"The boy with the golden hair, I think," said the lady, bending her large and wonderfully clear eyes on little Leum.

The upper sides of the carriage were chiefly of glass, so that the children could see another woman inside, whom they did not like so well.

This was a black woman, with a wonderfully long neck, hung round with many strings of large variously coloured beads, and on her head was a sort of turban of silk striped with all the colours of the rainbow, and fixed in it was a golden star.

This black woman had a face as thin almost as a death's-head, with high cheekbones, and great goggle eyes, the whites of which, as well as her wide range of teeth, showed in brilliant contrast with her skin, as she looked over the beautiful lady's shoulder, and whispered something in her ear.

"Yes; the boy with the golden hair, I think," repeated the lady.

And her voice sounded sweet as a silver bell in the children's ears, and her smile beguiled them like the light of an enchanted lamp, as she leaned from the window with a look of ineffable fondness on the golden-haired boy, with the large blue eyes; insomuch that little Billy, looking up, smiled in return with a wondering fondness, and when she stooped down, and stretched her jeweled arms towards him, he stretched his little hands up, and how they touched the other children did not know; but, saying, "Come and give me a kiss, my darling," she raised him, and he seemed to ascend in her small fingers as lightly as a feather, and she held him in her lap and covered him with kisses.

Nothing daunted, the other children would have been only too happy to change places with their favoured little brother. There was only one thing that was unpleasant, and a little frightened them, and that was the black woman, who stood and stretched forward, in the carriage as before. She gathered a rich silk and gold handkerchief that was in her fingers up to her lips, and seemed to thrust ever so much of it, fold after fold, into her capacious mouth, as they thought to smother her laughter, with which she seemed convulsed, for she was shaking and quivering, as it seemed, with suppressed merriment; but her eyes, which remained uncovered, looked angrier than they had ever seen eyes look before.

But the lady was so beautiful they looked on her instead, and she continued to caress and kiss the little boy on her knee; and smiling at the other children she held up a large russet apple in her fingers, and the carriage began to move slowly on, and with a nod inviting them to take the fruit, she dropped it on the road from the window; it rolled some way beside the wheels, they following, and then she dropped another, and then another, and so on. And the same thing happened to all; for just as either of the children who ran beside her caught the rolling apple, somehow it slipt into a hole or ran into a ditch, and looking up they saw the lady drop another from the window, and so the chase was taken up and continued till they got, hardly knowing how far they had gone, to the old cross-road that leads to Owney. It seemed that there the horses' hoofs and carriage wheels rolled up a wonderful dust, which being caught in one of those eddies that whirl the dust up into a column, on the calmest day, enveloped the children for a moment, and passed whirling on towards Lisnavoura, the carriage, as they fancied driving in the centre of it; but suddenly it subsided, the straws and leaves floated to the ground, the dust dissipated itself, but the white horses and the lackeys, the gilded carriage, the lady and their little golden-haired brother were gone.

At the same moment suddenly the upper rim of the clear setting sun disappeared behind the hill of Knockdoula, and it was twilight. Each child felt the transition like a shock—and the sight of the rounded summit of Lisnavoura, now closely overhanging them, struck them with a new fear.

They screamed their brother's name after him, but their cries were lost in the vacant air. At the same time they thought they heard a hollow voice say, close to them, "Go home."

Looking round and seeing no one, they were scared, and hand in hand—the little girl crying wildly, and the boy white as ashes, from fear, they trotted homeward, at their best speed, to tell, as we have seen, their strange story.

Molly Ryan never more saw her darling. But something of the lost little boy was seen by his former playmates.

Sometimes when their mother was away earning a trifle at haymaking, and Nelly washing the potatoes for their dinner, or "beatling" clothes in the little stream that flows in the hollow close by, they saw the pretty face of little Billy peeping in archly at the door, and smiling silently at them, and as they ran to embrace him, with cries of delight, he drew back, still smiling archly, and when they got out into the open day, he was gone, and they could see no trace of him anywhere.

This happened often, with slight variations in the circumstances of the visit. Sometimes he would peep for a longer time, sometimes for a shorter time, sometimes his little hand would come in, and, with bended finger, beckon them to follow; but always he was smiling with the same arch look and wary silence—and always he was gone when they reached the door.

Gradually these visits grew less and less frequent, and in about eight months they ceased altogether, and little Billy, irretrievably lost, took rank in their memories with the dead.

One wintry morning, nearly a year and a half after his disappearance, their mother having set out for Limerick soon after cockcrow, to sell some fowls at the market, the little girl, lying by the side of her elder sister, who was fast asleep, just at the grey of the morning heard the latch lifted softly, and saw little Billy enter and close the door gently after him. There was light enough to see that he was barefoot and ragged, and looked pale and famished. He went straight to the fire, and cowered over the turf embers, and rubbed his hands slowly, and seemed to shiver as he gathered the smouldering turf together.

The little girl clutched her sister in terror and whispered, "Waken, Nelly, waken; here's Billy come back!"

Nelly slept soundly on, but the little boy, whose hands were extended close over the coals, turned and looked toward the bed, it seemed to her, in fear, and she saw the glare of the embers reflected on his thin cheek as he turned toward her. He rose and went, on tiptoe, quickly to the door, in silence, and let himself out as softly as he had come in.

After that, the little boy was never seen any more by any one of his kindred.

"Fairy doctors," as the dealers in the preternatural, who in such cases were called in, are termed, did all that in them lay—but in vain. Father Tom came down, and tried what holier rites could do, but equally without result. So little Billy was dead to mother, brother, and sisters; but no grave received him. Others whom affection cherished, lay in holy ground, in the old church-yard of Abington, with headstone to mark the spot over which the survivor might kneel and say a kind prayer for the peace of the departed soul. But there was no landmark to show where little Billy was hidden from their loving eyes, unless it was in the old hill of Lisnavoura, that cast its long shadow at sunset before the cabin-door; or that, white and filmy in the moonlight, in later years, would occupy his brother's gaze as he returned from fair or market, and draw from him a sigh and a prayer for the little brother he had lost so long ago, and was never to see again.

WISH

Al Sarrantonio

C*hristmas.*

A baby-blanket of snow enfolded the earth, nuzzled the streets. Great lips of snow hung from gutters; caps of snow topped mailboxes and lampposts.

Christmas.

Dark green fir trees stood on corners, heavy with ornaments and blinking bulbs, dusted with silver tinsel that hung from each branch like angels' hair. Great thick round wreaths, fat red bows under their chins, hung flat against each door. Telephone poles sprouted gold stars; more lights, round, fat, and bright, were strung from pole to pole in parallel lines. The air, clean and cold as huffing breath, smelled of snow, was white and heavy and fat with snow.

Christmas.
Christmas was here.
It was April.

DAISY AND TIMOTHY HID tight in the cellar. Tied and dusty, April surrounded them in fly-specked seed packets, boxes of impotent tulip bulbs, rows of limp hoes and shovels. Spring was captured and caged, pushed flat into the ground and frozen over, coffined tight and dead.

Above them, out in the world, they heard the bells. A cold wind hissed past. The cellar window shadowed over as something slid past on the street.

Ching-ching-ching.

They held their breaths.

Ching-ching.

The window unshadowed; the hiss and bells moved away.

The bells faded to a distant rustle.

They breathed.

Timothy shook out a sob.

"Don't you touch me!" he bellowed when his sister put a hand on his shoulder. "It's your fault! All the rest are in that *place* because of you—don't you *touch* me!" He pushed himself farther back between two boxes marked "Beach Toys."

Outside, somewhere, a mechanical calliope began to play "Joy to the World."

Winter silence hung between them until Timothy said, "I'm sorry."

Daisy held her hand out to him, her eyes huge and lonely, haunted. He did nothing—but again when her fingers fell on his shoulder he recoiled.

"No! You wished it! It's your fault!"

Daisy hugged herself.

Timothy's face was taut with fright. "You said, 'I wish it was Christmas always! I wish this moment would last forever.' " He pointed an accusing hand at her. "I was there when you said it. By the fireplace, while we hung our stockings. I heard that voice too—*but I didn't listen to it!*" He pointed again. "*Why did you have to wish?*"

"I wish it was April! I wish it was spring!" Daisy screamed, standing up. An open carton of watermelon seeds, collected carefully by the two of them the previous summer, tilted and fell to the floor. Unborn watermelons scattered dryly everywhere. "It was just a voice, I don't know how it happened," she sobbed. "*I wish it was Spring!*"

Nothing happened.

Outside the frosted cellar window, the calliope finished "Joy to the World" and went without pause into "Silver Bells."

"You wished it and now you can't unwish it!" Timothy railed. "That voice is gone and now it will always be Christmas!"

Daisy's face changed—she ignored his squirming protest when she clamped her hand to his arm.

"Listen!" she whispered fiercely.

"I won't! It's your fault!"

"*Listen!*"

Her wild, hopeful eyes made him listen.

He heard nothing for a moment. There was only Christmas winter out there—a far-off tinkly machine playing Supermarket carols, the sound of glass ornaments pinging gently against one another on outdoor trees and, somewhere far off, the sound of bells.

But then there was something else.

Warm.

High overhead.

Blue and yellow.

A bird.

Daisy and Timothy raced for the window. Daisy got there first, but Timothy muscled her away, using the pulled cuff of his flannel shirt to rub-melt the frost from a corner of the rectangular glass. He put his eye to the hole.

Listened.

Nothing; then—

Birdsong.

He looked back at his sister, who pulled him from his peephole and glued herself to it. After a moment—

"I see it!"

Mountain-high overhead, a dark speck circled questioningly.

It was not a Christmas bird. It had nothing to do with Christmas. It was a spring bird, seeking April places—green tree branches and brown moist ground with fat red worms in it. A sun yellow and tart-sweet as lemons. Mown grass with wet odors squeezed out of each blade. Brown-orange baseball diamonds and fresh-black-topped playfields smelling of tar.

The bird whistled.

"April!" Timothy shouted.

He pulled frantically at the latch to the window, turning it aside and pulling the glass panel back with a winter groan. Cold air bit in at them. Snow brushed at their foreheads, danced and settled in their hair.

Timothy climbed out.

High up, whirling like a ball on a string, the bird cried.

"Yes! Yes! Spring!" Timothy yelled up at it.

Daisy climbed out beside him.

"You did it!" Timothy said happily. "You undid your wish!"

The cellar window snapped shut.

Something small plummeted.

Frozen white and silver, the bird fell into a soft death-coverlet of snow.

"It was a trick!" Timothy screamed. "What are we going to do?" He turned to the locked window, tried frantically to push it in. When he opened his mouth, puffs of frosted air came out with his words.

"We've got to get away!"

Timothy and Daisy looked to the horizon. A huge red ball was there, a second sun, an ornament a hundred stories high, and from it came the faint jangle of bells, the smooth snow-brushed sound of sleigh runners.

"We'll be brought to that place—we've got to get away!"

The sleigh bells, the glassy sound of sled-packed snow, grew toward them. Before Daisy's hands could find Timothy, could pull him against the side of the house, he tore away from her. The bells rose to a hungry clang; Daisy could almost hear them sing with pleasure.

Timothy's fading voice called back:

"Why did you listen to that voice . . . ?"

The bells grew very loud and then very soft, and moved away.

Christmas continued. In the sky, a few hearty snowflakes pirouetted and dropped. Tinsel shimmered on tree branches. The air stayed clean and cold, newly winterized. Balsam scent tickled the nostrils. Christmas lights glowed, blinked.

From the horizon, from the giant red Christmas ball, came a sound.

Bells.

Soft silver bells.

"No!" Daisy's feet carried her from the side of the house to the white-covered sidewalk. She left tiny white feet in a path behind her.

The bells belled.

Daisy ran.

The lazy bells followed her. Like a ghost's smoky hands, they reached out at her only to melt away and re-form. Daisy passed snow-white houses, with angels in the windows and mistletoe under the eaves.

Daisy stopped.

The bells hesitated. There came a tentative *ching*, followed by silence and then another *ching-ching*.

Daisy ran, her yellow hair flying.

The houses disappeared, replaced by a row of stores with jolly front windows and Christmas-treed displays. Lights blinked. Above one store a plastic Santa drawn by plastic reindeer rose, landed, rose, landed.

Ching-ching.

The library budded into view. White-coated brick, its crystal windows were filled with cutouts of Christmas trees and holly.

At the top of the steps, the doorway stood open.

Daisy climbed, entered.

Outside, the ghoul-bells chimed.

Ching-ching.

Ching-ching.

Ching.

She heard the smooth stop of sleigh-skis in the snow.

The library door loomed wide.

Someone stepped into it.

"Daisy?" a voice called coldly. It was a voice she knew.

"*Daisy?*" it spoke again. Icicles formed in the corners; snow sprinkled down from the ceiling. It was the voice that had spoken to her.

Daisy pushed past the empty librarian's desk, knocked over the silver Christmas tree on the counter. She dove under the tasseled red rope into the children's section. Bright book covers glared at her. Babar the elephant walked a tightrope; the bulb-like faces of Dr. Seuss characters grinned; Huckleberry Finn showed off his inviting raft to his hulking friend Jim. "I wish I could be with them," Daisy thought; but nothing happened.

Behind her, the voice, closer, called again in chilly singsong:

"Daisy, Daisy, it's Christmas always!"

"No!" Daisy hissed to herself fiercely. She crawled under one stack of books that had been left to spill against a bookcase, making an arch. Behind it were more books—Hardy Boys and Nancy Drews, two *Treasure Island*s, one *Robinson Crusoe* tilted at an angle. Behind them a pile of *National Geographic* magazines, with color covers.

Daisy burrowed her way into the magazines, covered herself with books and periodicals, made a fort of the Hardy Boys with a fortress gate made of The Wind in the Willows.

Steps clacked closer against the polished oak floor.

"Where are you?" the cold voice sang.

"Christmas all the time!"

"Always Christmas!"

"Daisy . . ."

The footsteps ceased.

The Hardy Boys were lifted away.

"Daisy . . ."

A hard hand reached down to fall on her. She felt how death-cold he was. His suit was red ice; he wore a red cap at a jaunty angle.

His face was white, his ice-blue eyes were arctic circles filled with swirling frost.

"I wish it was spring! I wish it was April!"

"Christmas always," he said, smiling a sharp blue smile.

"I wish I could kill you!"

With her two small hands Daisy threw *The Wind in the Willows* up at him. A corner of the book hit his cold, smoky eye and he staggered back.

Miraculously, amazingly, he fell. There was a shatter like an icicle hitting the sidewalk. There was the *ching* of a million tiny bells.

He lay silent.

He lay . . . dead.

Daisy got up to see a dying blizzard blowing in his eyes. A cold blue hand lifted momentarily, reached toward her—and fell back, cracking up and down its length.

He dripped melting water.

Daisy breathed.

Outside, a bird sang.

Daisy crawled under the book arch, under the red tassel. She ran past the empty desk, the fallen silver tree, out the yawning door.

The sky was growing blue. A squirrel ran past. A blackbird dipped low, squawked and didn't fall.

It was April.

Spring.

Christmas was leaving the world.

Balsam scent grew sour and stale. The snow grew old-gray and slushy. Winter was old; the house lights, round wreaths, tinsel grew dim and left-out-too-long. In the middle of "Have Yourself a Merry—" the calliope ground to a halt.

At the horizon, the huge red ball was less shiny-bright.

His sleigh stood in front of the library. It was ice-white and red, lined with ice bells, pulled by ice reindeer. It shivered as Daisy climbed into it and snapped the reins.

"Take me to them," she said.

The sleigh shuddered into melting life.

Spring was exploding around her. They went over miles of white earth turning to green. The air was warm as hay. Fish leaped in blue-clear ponds, orange-yellow flowers burst from the ground, leaves generated spontaneously. Daisy wondered if, back in her cellar, watermelons were sprouting everywhere and hoes and shovels were dancing up the stairs to reach the loamy soil.

Beneath Daisy, the ice sleigh dripped into the ground. The soil drank it up—bells, reindeer and all. Daisy leaped from the last puddle of it, new green grass like springs pushing at her feet.

Over a short hill, touching the spring sky—and there was the red ball.

It was a blown-glass Christmas bulb halfway up the sky. Its glossy crimson was tarnishing. Winter rushed out the tiny door at the bottom, howling, eaten alive by spring. Daisy hugged herself as it blew past.

The dying snowstorm engulfed her, pulled her inside.

She sobbed at what was there.

The ball was filled with frozen Christmas. A *Nutcracker* Christmas tree, with a thousand presents underneath, filled the center of the ball. Its branches sagged. Lights were everywhere, winking out. And lining the walls all the way to the top were frozen people keeping frozen Christmas.

A spidery white stairway wound up and around, and Daisy stepped onto it. There was the snap of melting ice. She looked in at each block, wiping warm tears of water away with her fingers. In one there was a man with a beard she knew who watered his lawn in the summer each Saturday, even if it rained. His beard was frozen now. He knelt before a Christmas tree, fitting it into its stand. There was a boy who delivered newspapers, caught removing a model airplane from its Christmas wrap. A woman was ice in her rocking chair, a mince pie cradled in her pot-holdered hands—the pie looked good enough to eat. A little girl made garlands out of popcorn. A mother and daughter exchanged Christmas cards.

At the end of the winding stair, at the very top, was—

Timothy.

Daisy gasped. Timothy stared out at her like wax. In his hand he held a limp, flat stocking; he bent to tack it to a rich-oiled mantel above a fireplace. A log fire burned snugly in the grate.

The ice shimmered and softened; Timothy moved.

Beside him, there was an empty space.

As Daisy reached out, the ice hardened again.

"Can't . . . unwish . . . ," Timothy said before his mouth froze closed.

Outside, she heard the bells.

Winter came rushing back. The air glinted like clear cold crystal. The tarnished ball grew metal-shiny. On the Christmas tree, limp pine boughs stiffened, grew tall. Nearby in the walls, in the air, the calliope played "God Rest Ye Merry, Gentlemen."

Ching-ching.

The sleigh moved over the snow with a sound like *wishhhhhhh.*

Ching.

Daisy looked up, and in the red metal glass above her, someone was reflected from far below.

Someone tall and white, with red-ice coat, blue-ice eyes, black-ice boots.

"Ice is water," he explained, in his voice; "water makes ice."

"I wished you were dead!" Daisy screamed.

He put his boot on the stair.

He climbed.

He stood before her.

As he finally put his cold hand on her; as she felt Christmas brighten and stiffen around her; as she felt the red velvet stocking caress her hands, and smelled the wood smoke from the fireplace, and felt Timothy's hand on her arm, telling her not to listen; as ice filled around her and hardened and froze her forever, she heard whispered close by, in a voice she now knew might have been any of a thousand cold or hot voices, a voice that might become any of a thousand cold or hot things, a laughing voice, a voice that was ancient, persistent and patient in its longing for release, "Make a wish."

THE THIRD NATION

Lee Hoffman

If she were the two-legged kind, he'd catch 'er quick enough." Grinning, Hull poked Dayton with an elbow.

"If she were that kind, I'd be there first," Dayton said.

Hull had a wad of tobacco in one cheek. He spat, and called, "Go get 'er, Lacey! Grab 'er by the trotter!"

Lacey was a big man, and muscled like a prime bull. Despite the chill, there was sweat beading on his forehead. He pushed back his kepi and wiped at it. Like the other Bummers, his face was stained from the smoke of pine knot fires. In the long morning light his breath was faintly visible. He'd already lunged for the pig four, five times, and it had scooted away every time. Now, backed up into the angle between an old outbuilding and a piece of rail fence, it eyed him warily.

The rest of the foragers had spread out behind Lacey to urge him on and watch the fun. If it had been a full-grown hog, the lieutenant would probably have given orders to shoot it rather than waste time running the lard off it, but it was a young one and from the look of it, it had been rooting wild instead of penned to fatten. So the lieutenant stood back and let the men enjoy a little sport.

"I'll get 'er this time," Lacey said. Again, he lunged.

Again, the pig scooted away. Frantic, it charged toward the wall of men.

Shouting and laughing, the men converged to head it off.

The pig wheeled and darted toward the end of the fence.

"Flank it, boys! Flank it!" the lieutenant called.

The pig turned again, this time heading straight at Cahill.

Cahill was the youngest one in the company. He looked more like a drummer boy than a fighting man, but he'd been blooded at Resaca. Now he took pride in being one of Sherman's Bummers. As it charged past him, he grabbed for the pig. His hands connected, but the pig squirmed out of his grip. Tail up, it headed across the overgrown pasture toward the woods.

"I'll get 'er!" Cahill lit out after the high-tailing pig.

Fun was fun, but pigs were food. The lieutenant shouted, "Shoot the damn thing before it gets away!"

Nash was the sharpshooter of the company. He'd got himself a breech-loading Spencer, and claimed he could cut the middle star out of a Rebel battle flag at a thousand yards. Slinging the rifle to his shoulder, he set his sights and called, "Leave 'er be, boy! I'll get 'er!"

Maybe Cahill didn't hear him, or maybe he was just too excited and set on making the capture. He kept going. But the pig was gaining ground fast. Nash had a clean line of sight. Leading the target, he closed his finger on the trigger.

As the hammer fell, the pig swerved. Dirt and grass spattered where the pig had been. But the pig was already racing into the woods. For all it was gaining on him, Cahill was still hard after it.

"Oh, hell," the lieutenant said.

Whooping as if it were a band of Rebs they were chasing, the rest of the company lit out after Cahill.

It would have been a poor place to chase a Reb who might shoot back but, as woods went, it was a pretty good one for hunting a pig. Although the pine and live oaks held their leaves all winter, in December much of the other foliage had browned and fallen, making a crisp mat on the ground. The undergrowth was mostly a tangle of bare branches. A man could see a good ways into the woods and could hear brogans crunching the fallen leaves. The pig flashed in and out of sight among the tree trunks. Cahill, in his dark blue field jacket and light trousers, stayed easily visible.

Hull saw the pig scramble over a windfallen tree and Cahill spring up with a foot on the tree trunk. Suddenly Cahill disappeared behind the tree and Hull heard a high sharp scream. He thought it was the pig squealing, that Cahill'd jumped it and caught it. But the scream stopped, and a caught pig usually kept squealing.

As he reached the windfall, he saw Cahill sitting on the ground, one leg stretched out in front of him. The other was drawn up and Cahill was hugging it tight, rocking a bit. Hull had seen men hug themselves and rock that way before, on the battlefield. Wounded men.

Dayton reached Cahill first and knelt beside him. The others came up, circling around him. Hull heard Cahill saying, " . . . think my leg's broke." His voice was hoarse with pain.

The lieutenant was last to arrive. As he loped up, Dayton told him, "Sir, Cahill's broke his leg."

Hull could see what had happened. The log was half rotten. There was a hole in the top where Cahill's foot had gone in and caught. Off balance, he'd fallen, wrenching his ankle.

"Let's see," the lieutenant said, gesturing for Dayton to reveal the wound.

Dayton dropped to one knee. With his penknife, he slit the trouser on Cahill's outstretched leg. When he peeled back the cloth, there was no sign of blood and the leg looked straight. It wasn't until he took hold of Cahill's brogan that Cahill grunted with pain. Gently, he removed the brogan. Wrinkling his nose, he said to Cahill, "Don't you ever wash your feet?"

Cahill managed with a weak grin, "I didn't know you were gonna be sniffing around them."

When Dayton had bared Cahill's leg and foot, the lieutenant moved him aside and knelt for a look. He ran a hand down Cahill's shin, then touched his ankle. Cahill fought against showing pain, but he couldn't hold back a couple of whimpers.

Finally, the lieutenant stood up again and wiped his hands. "I don't think there are any bones broken," he said.

Cahill looked disappointed. "I can't stand up."

"Oh, you're hurt all right," the lieutenant agreed. "I think your ankle's dislocated. We'll have to get you back to the surgeon."

"If that's all it is, I can fix it," Heinke said.

The lieutenant gave him a questioning frown.

Heinke explained, "My pop's a horse doctor, sir."

"It's work for a surgeon," the lieutenant said.

"Sooner it's done, the better," Heinke told him.

He hesitated. "If you're sure you can do it."

"Yes, sir!" Heinke said proudly. He looked at the men gathered around. "Couple of you fellers take hold of him, hold him tight."

"I'll do it." Setting down his musket, Lacey stepped behind Cahill and wrapped his arms around the boy's chest.

"What you gonna do?" Cahill asked.

Unspeaking, Heinke grabbed the boy's foot and tugged. Cahill screamed and then went limp.

"Oh, Lord!" Lacey whispered, bracing the boy in his arms. "He's died!"

"Passed out," Heinke said. "Best thing for him." He worked at the ankle a few moments longer, then sat back on his haunches and wiped his forehead. "I expect that'll fix it. But he ain't gonna be able to walk on it for a while."

There was sweat on the lieutenant's face, too. He drew a kerchief from a pocket and wiped at it. "Lacey, can you carry him?"

"Yes, sir."

"All right, you take him back to that farmhouse."

"What about the pig, sir?" Dayton asked.

The lieutenant gave a little laugh. "That pig'll be halfway to Savannah by now."

Dayton muttered. "I had my mouth all set for fresh pork."

"Don't worry, we'll find another one." The lieutenant turned back to Lacey. "Stay with him. Soon as we forage up a horse or mule, I'll send it back for you to carry him on to camp."

"Shouldn't somebody else go along with 'em, sir? In case those Reb deserters are around here somewhere?" Hull suggested. It had been several days since a planter'd told them about being robbed by Rebs running ahead of Sherman's march, and several days before that when it had happened. The odds were against them still being in the area, but Hull had a notion to go back and explore the empty farmhouse. When the Secesh ran off in a hurry, sometimes they left valuables behind.

The lieutenant nodded. "Go ahead. Keep a sharp eye out. I'll get somebody back to you as soon as I can."

Cahill was coming out of his faint. He choked back a groan as Lacey got him up over his shoulder like a blanket roll. Hull picked up Lacey's musket and they headed for the farmhouse.

The farm was an old one. When he got a good look at it Hull's hopes of loot sank. This place looked like it had been abandoned long before Sherman's Army left Atlanta in flames.

The house was built of rough-hewn planks that had weathered to a dreary gray. Rotting planks dangled from the walls. Patches of shakes had scabbed off from the roof as if it had an ugly disease. Both of the big brick chimneys flanking the house had lost their capping. Just a few sections of the rail fence still stood, and the smokehouse door gaped askew.

The only signs of life the foragers had seen when they first arrived were a bluejay perched on the porch roof and the pig that had been rooting around the empty corn crib. The bluejay had left when Lacey'd made his first lunge at the pig.

The jay was back when the returning men reached the house. It flew off again as Lacey set Cahill down on the edge of the porch. Cahill was keeping a diary. Once he was settled comfortably, he pulled it out and began scribbling. Lacey stretched out on his back with his hands under his head.

Hull stood a while, wondering whether he should suggest Lacey come with him. Together, they could look out for each other. But if he did find anything small enough to pocket, he didn't fancy sharing it. Finally, he gave the door a shove. It swung open.

"Uncle Billy's orders are to stay out of dwellings," Lacey called to him.

He looked back, cocking a brow at Lacey. Despite the orders, they'd gone foraging inside more than one Secesh house on this march. "It ain't hardly a dwelling if there's nobody *dwelling* in it, is it?"

Lacey's grin said he'd been joking. He added, "Remember, it's fair shares all around."

"I doubt there's anything in here but rat nests," Hull answered, hoping he was wrong. If it turned out he was, he had no intention of telling Lacey. Musket in hand, he stepped cautiously inside.

The room he entered was as damply chill as a springhouse. It was an odd kind of cold that smelled of musty decay. A graveyard cold. He tensed at a sound: a faint rustling, like the dry leaves in the woods. Rats in the walls, he told himself, that was all.

Ghosts of the dead that lurked in old houses were just tales for scaring children. If he'd ever believed in such things, he'd lost his faith on the battlefield. When a man died, what was left was cold meat, nothing more. He'd seen that for himself. If there was a spirit in a man, like the preachers claimed, it didn't linger once the body was dead. Of that, he was certain. Even so, he shivered at the feel of the place more than the chill. The house looked deserted, but somehow it just didn't feel empty.

The corners of the room were filled with shadows and cobwebs. There were old ashes in the hearth, and some shredded bits of a snakeskin rubbed off against the rough bricks. A few pieces of furniture not worth hauling off huddled in the shadows.

To his right was a half-open door. He peeked in: a battered old table and a couple of chairs, both missing splats. On the table were a stone jug, a chipped plate, and a dented tin ladle. But no cobwebs. He frowned at that. Rats didn't set out dishes. Did spooks? But there wasn't any such thing.

Warily, he peered around the room. There were plenty of cobwebs in the corners, and a pine cupboard hulked against one wall. Nothing else. He looked under the table. Nothing there. The cupboard sat flush to the floor. No room under it for anything to hide. No Rebs in here waiting to jump him.

He touched a finger to the tabletop. No dust. No dust on the jug or plate, either. How long would it take for a layer of dust to settle on the table? He wasn't sure. Maybe a few days? Whoever'd used that plate was probably halfway to Savannah by now, he told himself. Didn't even have to have been a Reb. Could have been a runaway slave or a hunter taking shelter.

He picked up the jug and sniffed hopefully at its contents. Molasses. He set down the jug and went to the cupboard. Inside he found a few pieces of battered crockery, two shriveled sweet potatoes, and several pine cones. The pine cones puzzled him.

He thought about it all for a moment, then grinned. Didn't need to have been a Reb or hunter or slave. Could have been children playing house. That would explain the pine cones.

Even so, he edged open the back door slowly and stood back as he thrust out the barrel of his musket. Nobody took a shot at it. He chanced poking his head out. Nobody shot at it, either. Relieved, he looked around.

There was a small building with a large chimney about twenty feet behind the house. That'd be the kitchen, he supposed. It seemed the Secesh had a custom of putting their kitchens a ways from their houses. Someone had told him it was to keep down the damage when the kitchen caught fire.

Holding the musket ready, he crossed the yard. He used the muzzle to push open the kitchen door. A smell of rot hit him in the face. Rats scurried wildly for cover as light spilled through the doorway. Nobody in there, he thought. At least nobody alive. Likely nothing fit to forage, either. He pulled the door shut again and returned to the house.

Not enough molasses left in that jug to make it worth carrying, and those sweet potatoes were too old and dry. He started back through the parlor.

Abruptly he halted. There'd been no sound. Nothing to grab his attention, except a feeling. A sudden sense of something wrong.

He was at the bottom of the stairs. The staircase pressed tight against one wall as it rose through an opening in the ceiling. He looked up. There was a window at the head of the stairs. Grimy shards of glass hung in the frame. The sun was high enough now to throw jagged streaks of light through the holes. Dust danced in the beams, but no cobwebs ensnared them.

Whoever'd been in the house had gone upstairs. Might still be up there, he thought. He scanned the parlor, assuring himself it was still empty, and checked to be sure his musket was still capped. Climbing the stairs, he set each foot carefully at the wall side of the tread to keep it from squeaking.

Before his head reached the level of the floor above, he pulled off his kepi and balanced it on the musket barrel, then thrust it up through the passageway.

Nothing happened.

Cautiously, he took another step, looked out onto the second-floor landing. No Rebs crouched in the shadows.

Not even a small spook waving its winding sheet at him. He grinned sourly at himself for even thinking of ghosts.

There was a door to either side of the landing. Both were closed. Neither was sealed with cobwebs. He climbed onto the landing and decided to try the right-hand door first. He turned the knob slowly, then used the gun muzzle to nudge the door open. As it moved, the room breathed out the odors of decay and he could hear sounds of scurrying.

It had been a bedroom. The bedframe was gone, but an old tick lay crumpled on the floor, leaking mildewed straw through a dozen or more holes. He glimpsed a stringy gray tail disappearing into one. A litter of droppings confirmed that he'd found a rat's nest all right.

A massive clothes cupboard stood against the wall, its doors hanging open. The long-dry bones of a dead rat nestled in one corner. The skull was facing toward him, its empty sockets seeming to stare in surprise at his sudden appearance. He backstepped and closed the door.

Behind him, something squeaked.

He wheeled.

The door he faced was like the one he'd just turned away from. He stood for a moment, staring at it, listening. He could hear nothing. The noise had been another rat, he told himself. The place was full of rats.

He turned the knob, then pushed the door gently with the gun muzzle. Rusty hinges moaned as it swung open. An old clothes cupboard stood against one wall and a featherbed lay on the floor, but these furnishings did not look abandoned. The cupboard was shut and the featherbed spread out. A quilt was spread over the featherbed, And someone was under it.

The musty stink of the room was tinged with another odor, an ugly sickly odor he'd smelled often enough before.

"You there," he snapped at the quilt-covered figure on the featherbed, but he didn't really expect an answer. Not with that smell in the air. He took a step toward the body under the quilt, meaning to prod it with his musket and assure himself it was dead.

He stopped short at sight of the face. He'd recognized the outhouse stink of death, death that had been working for days, and he'd been prepared for the sight of it. Since he'd got into this war, he'd seen dead men aplenty. The sight no longer bothered him. Sometimes they'd died in horrible ways, sometimes with faces half shot off or rotted off by the time he saw them. But on the field it was always men.

This was a woman. A young woman with sorrel hair, undone and combed into a halo radiating from the splotched pallor of her face. Parchment skin molded into a taut image of the bone beneath, as if the flesh between had melted and flowed away. The mouth was open, lips drawn back in a silent mocking leer.

She hadn't died there all alone. That was damned sure. Someone had been there to close her eyes. On the lid of each was a three-dollar Federal gold piece.

He squatted to take them. As his fingers closed on one, he heard a squeak behind him. A voice struck him like a minié ball, jerking him to his feet, spinning him around. He saw the cupboard door now open and a face staring at him from inside.

"You leave my mama alone!" she screeched.

He scowled in amazement as the child lunged out of the cupboard. She was a scrawny, dirty-faced tow head. Her filthy rumpled dress was flounced with tattered lace and there were holes in stockings that looked like silk.

"You put that back!" She indicated the coin between his fingers.

Shaken, he said, "She's your ma?"

The girl nodded and repeated, "Put that back!"

He looked at the coin, then at the corpse. "Your ma's dead."

"I know that. She's gone to heaven to be with Papa, same as Grandma went to be with Grandpa," the girl said. "You give her back that there penny."

"She don't need it now."

"Does, too!"

"What for? You said she's gone to heaven."

She nodded.

"Well, the streets are paved with gold up there, ain't they? She won't miss no couple of—" he grinned slightly as he used her description "—pennies."

"Dead people gotta have pennies. They always do."

"No, they don't." He bent to scoop up the other coin. And saw the dull gleam of gold at the dead woman's throat. Nudging back the quilt, he found a lavaliere of gold set with a stone as big as his thumbnail and as red as fresh blood. His fingers clamped around it, snatching, breaking the fragile chain it hung from.

"That's my mama's do-pretty!" the girl protested.

He held up the lavaliere, letting it dangle from his fingertips. The red jewel was set into gold filigree. There was enough sunlight to set sparks flashing within the jewel. This was something worth foraging for, he thought. Hell, it was likely worth more than a foot soldier's pay for the whole war. Maybe enough to buy a partnership in a nice little saloon.

"What's the dead need with such things?" he said as much to himself as to the child.

"I don't know," she admitted, "but Grandma got buried with all hers."

He looked from the jewels to the girl. "All hers?"

"She had a lot of rubies." She pointed at the stone. "That's what I'm named after. Ruby. Grandma had a whole big string of them. Mama said she wore them when she got buried."

Hull stared at the child. Was she telling the truth? A whole string of rubies would be worth a fortune. Set a man up for life. He said, "Ain't so."

"Yes it is!"

"Where would your grandma get something like that?"

"Mama said she brought them with her when she come over from France. Mama said Grandma had to run away from the bad men who stole her plantation in France, and she brought all her do-pretties here with her so the bad men wouldn't get them, too. Grandma loved her do-pretties so much Papa put them on her when they buried her. That's what Mama said. She said she wished he hadn't done that."

Hull grinned, thinking it was a damnfool thing to do. A waste for such things to lie in a grave when the living could be making good use of them. He said, "Ruby, do you know where they buried your grandma?"

"You give Mama back her pennies."

"Here." He handed her the coins.

"And her do-pretty."

"You tell me about your grandma first. Where did they bury her?"

"In the churchyard," she said as she returned the coins to the eyelids of the corpse.

"What churchyard? Where?"

She scowled at him as if that were a foolish question. "Next to the church."

"Is it close by here? Can you show me?"

Her expression told him she thought that was another foolish question. "It's back home."

"This ain't your home?"

"Course not. We wouldn't live in no place like this. Only the Yankees was coming and we was going to Savannah only Mama took sick and we came here and the bad men came and we hid and they took our horse and cart and Mama died and I can't find nothing to eat but molasses and old dried-up sweet taters and you better give my mama back her do-pretty." As the words spilled out of her, tears trickled down her cheeks, drawing pale tracks through the dirt. Blinking, she gazed at him with a deep sadness. "You're a bad man, too, ain't you?"

"No, sugar, I ain't a bad man. I'm just a sodjer trying to get along in the world," he said, feeling sorry for the poor child. But not sorry enough to give up the lavaliere. "I don't mean you any harm, but I got a lot better use for this do-pretty than your mama—"

"Hull!" Lacey hollered from below. "Where are you? You all right?"

"Dammit," he mumbled under his breath. Over his shoulder, he shouted, "I'm all right. I'll be right down."

"I'm coming up," Lacey called back. "You found anything?"

"Who's that?" the girl asked.

"My friend," he said, but at that moment he didn't feel like Lacey was a friend at all. If Lacey saw that lavaliere, he was going to want a share, he thought as he stuffed it into a pocket. If Lacey saw the girl, he'd want to know what she was doing there. She was sure to tell him about the jewel. She was already opening her mouth like she was about to holler.

Hull wrenched her around, slamming a hand across her mouth, wildly hunting a way to keep her quiet. He could hear Lacey's brogans on the stairs. He had to keep Lacey from discovering her. He could think of only one way. Knotting a fist, he smashed it into the child's head.

The blow knocked her out all right. Hurriedly, he shoved her limp body into the cupboard and pushed the door closed. But as he let go, it started to swing open again. He pushed it back and turned the latch on it. Lacey's steps were close. As Hull snatched up the coins from the dead woman's eyes, he heard a board creak on the landing.

Then Lacey was at the doorway. He wrinkled his nose. "What the hell you found?"

"A dead woman," Hull said tautly, the coins clenched in the fist at his side. He shoved the fist into his pocket.

Lacey walked into the room and looked down at the corpse. "Poor thing. What you suppose happened?"

"She came in here and died."

"But how come?"

"How the hell should I know?"

Lacey shrugged.

Darting a look at the cupboard, Hull thought he'd better get Lacey away before the little girl woke up and began raising a racket. He said, "Least we can do is bury her decent like proper Christians."

"What about her people?"

"If she had people around here, don't you think they'd have taken care of her? Not left her here like this?"

"I guess so."

"We can roll her up in the featherbed. You take the bottom. I'll get the top." Hull started folding the side of the bed over the body.

A bit hesitantly, Lacey began to help. As he lifted his end, he said, "I don't much like dead people."

"Nobody does," Hull said. "That's why they bury 'em."

"Huh?"

"Come on, it stinks in here."

They carried the bundle down the stairs and through

the parlor. Cahill was watching the door. As they walked out onto the porch, he asked what had happened.

"Found a dead body. Gonna bury it," Hull grunted. If the girl began to holler when she woke up, would her voice carry this far? He asked Cahill, "Can you walk yet?"

"I can't even wiggle my foot."

"Come on," he said to Lacey, and he headed for the steps.

"Set her down a minute. I got to get another grip."

"It's a woman?" Cahill asked as they put the bundle down.

"It was once," Hull snapped, impatient to be on away from the house. He turned to Lacey. "I'll carry her. You bring Cahill."

"What? Why?"

"We want to give her a proper decent Christian burying, don't we? It wouldn't be respectful if Cahill didn't come, would it?"

"I don't think—" Cahill began.

Hull cut him short. "It's the least we can do as good Christians, ain't it?"

"I guess so," Lacey allowed.

Cahill shrugged.

Hull started trying to gather the bundle up in his arms. It wasn't heavy, but the featherbed was bulky, awkward. Seeing he was having trouble with it, Lacey suggested, "I'll help you and come back for Cahill."

"No, I'll get her all right," Hull said.

Cahill asked, "Where you gonna put her?"

"Away from the house," Hull replied. "A decent distance, in case anybody wants to move in here again."

"Move into *this* place?" Lacey said doubtfully.

Hull's impatience was turning to anger. He stopped himself from snapping at Lacey. Struggling to keep his voice calm and reasonable, he said, "Somebody must own it. They might want to fix it up someday."

"I suppose so." Lacey sounded doubtful, but willing to give in rather than argue. He looked at Hull struggling to pick up the bundle. "I'd better help you."

"No!"

Cahill frowned with puzzlement at Hull's insistence. He started to speak, stopped, held up a hand. "Listen."

Hull heard the sound: the jangle and rattle of a wagon. Wheeling, he saw it on the track to the house. The team was a pair of mismatched mules. They pulled a farm wagon loaded with sacks and casks. Heinke was driving, and Yates was at his side.

"There!" Lacey said happily, "Here come the fellers. They can help us with her."

"Yeah," Hull muttered, feeling the way the cornered pig must have felt with its back to the fence and the circle of men closing in around it.

As the wagon jounced up, Yates swung himself from the seat and strode toward the porch. Toward the bundle lying on it. "What you got there? Something good?"

"A dead woman," Lacey told him.

He stopped short. "You killed a woman?"

"We found her dead. We was gonna take her and bury her proper."

Heinke halted the mules. "Load up and let's get going."

"They got a dead woman here," Yates told him before Lacey could. But then he had to leave it to someone else to explain. Lacey was eager to talk. Hull stayed silent, letting Lacey tell all he knew about it.

Heinke and Yates agreed that the woman should be given a Christian burial, but Heinke thought they ought to take the corpse on to the camp and let an officer make the final decision. Yates wanted to go on the way Hull had proposed and make a grave for her in the woods. Lacey sided with Heinke. Cahill wasn't so sure, not that he disagreed about the burial, but he didn't like the idea of riding back to camp in the wagon with the corpse. Despite its wrappings, its odor was very evident.

"Stinking or not," Heinke said, "we got to take her with us. Might be there's something on her will tell who she is so's somebody can get in touch with her kin. You want to search her here, or let a surgeon do it?"

Nobody wanted to examine the corpse. They agreed to take it back and let an officer deal with the problem.

Hull didn't care, as long as they got away from the house before somebody discovered the child in the cupboard. Really ought to let her out before he left, he thought. At least open the latch so she'd be able to get herself out.

Patting a pocket, he started for the door. "You fellers load her up. I'll be right back. I've left my tobaccer in there somewhere."

"Wait a minute," Heinke snapped. "You and Lacey found her. *You* load her up while me and Yates get Cahill on board."

"But my tobaccer—"

"Forget your damned tobaccer. I'll give you a chaw of mine. Let's get the hell going before she gets any riper."

Hull started to argue, but if he did they might begin wondering if there was something more than just a lost plug he wanted from in the house. Sucking breath between his teeth, he glanced up, as if he hoped to see through walls and floor into the bedroom, into the cupboard. There was nothing he could do about it. Not lest he wanted to risk losing the jewel, and maybe his hide.

Sighing, he turned to help Lacey gather up the bundled corpse and heft it into the wagon bed.

Despite the pain in his ankle, Cahill refused to ride in the back, so they manhandled him up into Yates's place on the seat. Heinke swung up next to him and slapped the mules into motion. The others fell in behind.

Hull fought the urge to look back. The skin felt drawn taut around his ears. He could hear a jay squawking somewhere in the trees. And something else. A faint pounding—as of small hands hammering against a cupboard door? Or was it only the blood beating in his ears?

Thrusting a hand into his pocket, he clutched the jewel. What was done was done, he told himself. Think about what he was going to do, when he'd turned that do-pretty into cold hard cash. Hell, she was only a damned Secesh whelp, anyway. What did it matter what happened to her?

FOR A MAN WITH coin to clink, there was always liquor to be had somewhere among the troops. Hull had the coin. He got himself thoroughly drunk that night, and again the next. The lieutenant had to know about the liquor, but he was no deacon. As long as his men did their job and didn't make trouble for him, he didn't make trouble for them. Despite the intensity of his hangovers, Hull managed to do his job. With the aid of the whiskey, he managed to wash the unwanted memories into far dark corners of his mind.

From the time they'd taken Atlanta, there'd been very little fighting, mainly brief skirmishes with militia. They found fresh earthworks near Ogeechee Church, but the Rebs had abandoned them instead of making a stand. Savannah, though, proved fortified and defended. General Sherman himself had ridden out a railroad cut for a look and almost got his head knocked off by a Rebel cannonball. So the army encamped, eating rice and tearing up railroad track, while Hazen led the 15th Corps down the Ogeechee River and captured Fort McAllister.

Union ships began bringing supplies up the river to the army, and the engineers got busy providing roads to haul them on. There was a little skirmishing and some artillery fire on both sides, but nothing serious. It began to look like Sherman was planning to settle in for the winter and starve the Rebs out of Savannah.

Then, a few days before Christmas, a buggy full of aldermen came driving out from Savannah to surrender the city. Recognizing that a stand would be futile, the Reb troops had stretched pontoon bridges across the river and evacuated up an old plank road on the South Carolina side. So Sherman's forces marched into Savannah with their muskets over their shoulders.

Off duty at last, Hull, Dayton, Lacey, and Thorne drifted together to the waterfront. Savannah sat atop a high bluff overlooking the river. Wharves and warehouses lined the street at the foot of the bluff. Where there was shipping, and much coming and going, there were always places where a man with hard money could get a decent cup of whiskey, a game of chance, and the kind of company a soldier wanted after long months of campaigning. It didn't take long to find one.

Chuck-a-luck was Hull's game and luck was with him, or maybe the dark-eyed young waiter-woman who brought drinks at his beck brought him luck as well. In no time at all, he had doubled his money.

The thrill of the winning and the whiskey burned in his veins. When the dice turned against him, he thought it was only a momentary setback, and he bet with all the more furor. It was like a fever, growing hotter and hotter. The more he lost, the more he bet.

He called for the waiter-woman to bring the bottle and stay by his side while he rolled the dice. He didn't notice when Thorne disappeared upstairs with one of the female waiters, or when Dayton disappeared with another. When Lacey tried to pull him away from the board, he only cursed, emptied his glass, and went on playing.

This time the dice paid him. With a whoop of joy, certain his luck was back, he swept his winnings to his side of the board. The waiter-woman refilled his glass and took payment from the coins piled in front of him. He didn't notice how much she took. Lacey watched another throw. Hull won again. Shaking his head sadly, Lacey left.

As the night wore on, other players left, until only three soldiers and two civilians remained at the table. Again, the dice turned against Hull. The pile of coins before him dwindled. His gold three-dollar pieces were gone. His coppers followed, one after another until every cent he'd had was gone. The hell of it was that he felt certain—absolutely certain—that his luck would come back with the next roll. But without something to bet, there would be no next roll. And no trip upstairs with the dark-eyed waiter-woman.

It wasn't until he'd awakened the next day, sad and sober, that Hull remembered the ruby lavaliere. It was rolled up in a rag, stitched inside his jacket, waiting for him to return north again, to a prosperous place where he could find someone with hard money enough to pay him what it was worth. But he still had the feeling his luck was waiting on just one more roll of the dice. He had to lay hands on some coin somehow.

There was a way. He pondered it a while. He didn't know Savannah, and he didn't trust the Secesh. Slaves, though, were grateful to the army that had freed them. Some of them were so grateful they volunteered for the Pioneer Corps. That seemed a likely place to get the information he wanted.

A broad-shouldered buck who had been a stevedore knew where to find the pawnbroker with which his former owner had done business.

The place the freedman directed him to was a ramshackle wooden cottage that looked as old as the city. There was a brick warehouse crowding it on one side without quite touching it. On the other side, weeds were overgrowing the charred timbers of a building long gone. Rats scrabbled in the weeds.

The windows of the house were shuttered. The roof sagged over the meager porch and the single chimney leaned at a precarious angle. In the long winter twilight, the place looked abandoned.

Memories Hull had pushed away stirred like waking snakes in the shadowy corners of his mind. He fought them back, refusing to recognize them, but the feeling of them squirmed coldly down his spine as he approached the house. His steps slowed. The chill within him whispered that this couldn't be the right place. Nobody with hard money would live in such a place, he thought. Nobody with any choice would. Plantation slaves had better cabins than this.

As he stood pondering, a twist of smoke rose from the chimney. Somebody was inside. Maybe somebody who could tell him where to find the pawnbroker. He stepped up onto the porch. Boards groaned under his weight. As he reached out to knock, the door opened. A man who looked as old as the house peered out at him.

Startled, he backstepped.

"Don' worry, yankee. I don' bite." The old man's words were misshapen, his voice hardly more than a rattling in his throat. He grinned, lips drawing back from barren gums. "Wha' you want here?"

"I'm looking for a Mr. Hornbeck," Hull said. "Can you tell me where to find him?"

"Wha' you want with him?"

"Business."

"Who sent you?" He snapped the words out like an officer giving orders.

Automatically, Hull answered. "Cap'n Jarrett's Willy."

The old man gazed at him from shadowed hollows like empty eye sockets. "You know Jarrett?"

"I know Willy. He's joined the Pioneers."

"A better man than Jarrett," the old man mumbled. He stepped back, opening the door wider. "Come on inside."

Hull looked past him into a room lit only by a small hearth fire. Doubtfully, he said, "Hornbeck's here?"

"Better man than you, too," the old man added under his breath. Aloud, he said, "Who the devil do you think you're talkin' to?"

"You're Hornbeck?"

"I ain't gonna live forever. Come inside and state your business, or go 'way and leave me have my supper while I'm still spry enough to swaller it."

Hull thrust a hand into his pocket. His fingers located his Barlow knife and closed around it. Wishing he had his musket with him, he stepped inside.

Hornbeck lit a lamp and turned the flame high. That was a lot better. Hull glanced around. There seemed to be only the one room, and some kind of loft reached by a ladder. He saw a small bed behind the ladder and a comfortable-looking chair drawn up near the fire. Two side chairs faced each other across a table in front of the hearth. The walls were lined with sideboards, cupboards, chests, and cabinets, no two alike. Unless somebody was hiding in one of them, Hornbeck was alone. Hull's grip on the knife eased a bit.

Hornbeck had been cooking something over the hearth. He swung the pothook out to clear the fire, then opened a sideboard and took out a bottle. He set it and a pair of glasses on the table. Hull watched him pour. The golden brown whiskey shimmered invitingly in the lamplight. With a gesture, Hornbeck told him to help himself.

He picked up a glass and tasted the whiskey. It was the smooth, rich, sipping kind, but Hull took a long deep swallow. The heat of it in his throat thawed the chill in his spine.

"Sit down," Hornbeck said, seating himself at the table. "Show me what you've got."

Hull reached into his jacket and brought out the rag-wrapped bundle. Peeling back the rags, he sat the lavaliere on the table in front of him.

The admiration and pure greed that flashed in Hornbeck's eyes was as bright as the reflected lamplight that flashed in the ruby's heart. The old man reached out bony fingers and closed them gently on the lavaliere. He held it close to his face, studying it, turning it to catch the light. Softly, he asked, "For sale or pawn?"

"Pawn," Hull said. "How much?"

Hornbeck eyed him as intently as he'd studied the lavaliere. Setting it down on the table, he replied, "Ten dollars."

Hull snatched it. "You're crazy!"

"Gold," Hornbeck added.

"Willy told me you were fair!" Hull said as he started up from his seat. His fists clenched. He had a mind to show this old man what he thought of the offer.

Hornbeck shook his head. "I'm not fair. I'm hones'."

"Huh?"

"You take tha' to some other pawnbroker, maybe he'll offer you as much as a third of what it's worth, and when you go back for it maybe he and it will be gone the devil knows where. You wanna pawn it, you can be sure I'll keep it as long as we agree on, and I'll give it back to you for the amount we agree on. Tha's hones'. You *are* plannin' on comin' back for it, ain't you?"

"Damn right I am! I'll be back for it tomorrow."

"Then take wha' I offer. The less you take, the less it'll cost you to get it back."

Hull had never looked at it that way. It made a kind of sense. But ten dollars just didn't seem like enough, even in gold. As he thought about it, he emptied the whiskey glass.

"You know another hones' pawnbroker in Savannah?" Hornbeck asked as he refilled it.

Hull had to admit to himself that he didn't. He thought some more and drank some more. Finally, he said. "Fifty dollars."

"I thought you said you'd be comin' back for it."

"I will."

"You go spend fifty dollars now, tha's—wha'?—near four months' pay for you? Where you gonna get the money to pay me back?"

"How much you gonna charge me for the pawn?"

"Quarter a month."

"Quarter-eagle?" Hull said, thinking that wasn't so bad.

"Quarter the amount," Hornbeck told him. "If I was to len' you fifty—which I ain't gonna do—you'd owe me sixty-two and a half dollars nex' month."

"You sure ain't fair!"

"If I only len' you ten, all you'll owe me nex' month is twelve and a half."

The old man was right. Still, ten dollars just didn't seem like enough. Hull said so.

Hornbeck shrugged.

Feeling put upon, Hull said, "Forty?"

Hornbeck filled his glass again and waited until he'd drunk from it before speaking. "You said you'd come back for it tomorruh?"

"Yeah."

"I'll make a deal with you, sodjer. I'll len' you twen'y-five in gold and you come back with it tomorruh, like you say, I won't charge you nothin' for the loan. But if you don't come back for it tomorra, that pretty red do-pretty is all mine."

That wasn't fair either, Hull thought. But the confidence in him was as strong and warm as the whiskey he'd drunk. He didn't doubt luck would be with him at the dice table. He said, "You'll give me a paper says all that?"

"I surely will."

They drank to the agreement. Then Hornbeck sent Hull to wait on the porch. Hull took the lavaliere with him. After a few minutes, Hornbeck came to the door and put six coins into Hull's outstretched hand. Four quarter-eagles and three half-eagles. He waited patiently while Hull tested each with his teeth.

Satisfied the coins really were gold, Hull gave over the lavaliere and Hornbeck gave him the receipt.

It was full dark and turning cold by the time Hull reached the gambling house. Half a dozen of his friends were already there, at the board. They looked surprised to see him. Even more surprised when he put a quarter-eagle on the table.

"Where you been?" Lacey asked him.

Dayton asked, "Where'd you get that?"

"Foraging," Hull said with a grin.

The others laughed.

The civilian who had the dice cup looked down at the coin, up at Hull, then off to one side. In a moment, the dark-eyed waiter-woman appeared at Hull's side with a drink.

Just as he'd anticipated, Hull won on the first toss of the dice. And the second. And again. His luck was back, just the way he'd known it would be. He was sure of it. Exuberantly, he downed his drink and called for another.

On the fourth roll, he lost, but on the fifth he won again. Well, a man couldn't expect to win *every* time, no matter how good his luck was.

The luck stayed with him until the pile of coins in front of him was glittering with gold. With such luck, he ought to buy a partnership in a gambling house instead of a saloon, he thought. The way he was raking in the money, he wouldn't have to settle for a partnership. With all this money *and* the lavaliere, he could have a whole business for himself.

When the waiter-woman brought another drink, he wrapped his arm around her waist and pulled her close, rubbing his cheek against her hip. Warm and soft and so good-smelling. He felt like running her upstairs right that minute. But the clank of money drew his attention back to the chuck-a-luck board.

The woman stayed there until he was ready for another drink. When she walked away, it was like she took his luck with her. The dice turned against him. He called her back, but that didn't help. His heap of coins was shrinking fast.

The faster it went, the harder he bet. He cursed and pushed the woman away. He wanted no distraction. He had to win back the gold. He had to have twenty-five dollars when he left the table—it wasn't just a little money riding on the dice—it was a ruby lavaliere—it was his saloon—his future.

Breathing hard, sweating, his eyes were intent on the board, the coins, the dice. He watched the civilian's long sharp fingers rake up the coins that should have been his—that had been his moments before.

Again. And again.

And then there were no coins left. Nothing.

But the feeling was there, the certainty that he could win on the next roll. That he *would* win. His luck had to come back. His mistake had been sending the waiter-woman away, he thought. He'd been lucky when she was at his side, hadn't he?

Desperately, he looked around for his friends he might be able to borrow from. They were gone.

His money was gone. His glass was empty. Even the waiter-woman was gone.

He turned to the nearest man in Federal blue. They were comrades in arms, weren't they? A long way from home, among strangers, among enemies. They had to stick together, didn't they? Surely the soldier would help out a fellow with a small loan. Just a few cents.

The soldier only laughed.

He asked another and got shoved away, called a *stinking drunk.*

As he started toward a third, a civilian in shirt-sleeves laid a hand on his arm. "Friend, I think it's time for you to get back to camp."

"I jus' need a few coppers," Hull whined, "jus' len' me enough to get back in the game. I'll win nex' time. I know I will."

"You stop pesterin' the payin' customers. Go get some more money somewheres else if you wanna get back in the game," the civilian told him.

"But—"

"Now you go on." The man's fingers tightened on his arm, digging in, hurting. Hull realized then that the man was as big as Lacey, and probably as strong. Likely he could crush bone with those fingers. Still pleading, he let himself be led to the door. The man gave him a shove and slammed the door behind him.

As he started down the steps, his foot slipped and suddenly he was tumbling, slamming face-first into the cobbled walk. He lay still, his mouth filling with the salt taste of blood, his face filled with pain.

When he finally pulled himself up, he realized he was shivering. Realized it was cold. Very cold. And very dark.

There was a lamp flickering at the corner. He staggered toward it. As he passed the protection of the corner building, a damp ugly wind hit him, cutting through his field jacket. Felt like the blood that seeped from his nose was freezing in his moustache. Wasn't supposed to get so cold in the South, was it? But there was ice skinned over the puddles in the gutters. Have to watch his step. He pressed a hand against the wall to steady himself. Had to think. Needed money. Had to get that lavaliere back.

He remembered Hornbeck's shack. The old man had been alone there. Not even a dog. Nothing there but a shriveled up old man and a ruby lavaliere. And a lot of money hid somewhere. Old bastard had no business asking a quarter a month for a loan. Damn thief. Would serve him right if he got foraged.

But where the hell was the shack? Which direction was which? He'd turned the corner and got turned around somehow. The stars were no help. A black sky was bellied down on the treetops, not blinking so much as a single star.

Wind'd be off the river, wouldn't it? Felt like it. The shack had been near the river. He headed into the wind.

As he walked, his mind drifted. On a long march a man could learn to sleep after a fashion while he was walking. Not really sleep, but an unawareness that was close to it.

Suddenly he realized he wasn't walking into the wind any longer. There was icy rain in the wind now, and he had his back to it. He had been drifting like an animal ahead of a blizzard.

Where the hell was he?

It was too dark to tell. Felt like grass under his feet. That didn't help much. Savannah was full of grassy squares. He hunkered down. Shielding it against the wind with his body, he struck a sulphur match. It flared just long enough for him to glance around, then sputtered out.

In that quick glance, he'd seen odd shapes. Low shapes. Upright slabs. Low structures. He struck another match.

Goddamn!

Tombstones. He was in a graveyard.

He felt a sudden shivering down his spine, as if snakes were squirming through it. Snakes of memory refused by the mind.

But a graveyard was no different from a field after battle, except there was dirt and markers over the dead, he told himself. He'd had truck enough with the dead in the past. He didn't fear them now. Fact was, the dead had done well by him. It was a dead woman who'd given him the lavaliere.

Remembering that, he remembered the little girl telling him her grandma had been buried wearing even finer jewels. He didn't want to remember the child. But the jewels. That was worth thinking about. He'd heard tales of graverobbers finding gold rings on corpses. No telling what the dead of Savannah got buried wearing.

He figured this was the same graveyard he'd seen by daylight a few days before. An old place, going back to

Colonial times. Not everybody in it had been buried under six feet of dirt. Some were in brick vaults.

Dead people lived good around here, he thought. The vaults were bigger than a dog tent and sure to be a lot snugger in foul weather. If anybody was to get buried wearing fancy jewelry, seemed likely it'd be the people in those vaults. If a man could get into one, no telling what he'd find.

He tried lighting another match, but the weather-damp head crumbled when he struck it. Only two matches left in the case. Best not waste them. Moving cautiously in the darkness, he groped for stone. His fingers numbed quickly in the icy wind. The rain had soaked his uniform. His whole body was going numb. But the thought of the ruby kept him going.

He found a vault by blundering into it, hitting his thigh against a corner so abruptly that it sent him sprawling. Mumbling under his breath, he got himself up and began examining the structure with his hands. It was a low brick enclosure with a slab of marble for a top. From the weathered roughness of the marble, it was old. He gripped the top and pulled. Heavy. He pulled again. It still wouldn't move. He got down on one knee and tried pushing up on it. Too damned heavy. He couldn't budge it at all.

Sitting back on his heels, he pondered the situation. Had to be some way to get the damn thing open. If he couldn't get the top off, maybe he could get in from the side.

He ran his hands over the bricks. The mortar between them crumbled into sand under his fingers. Hunting the Barlow knife from his pocket, he began to pick at the mortar.

It didn't take long. The brick he was working at began to wobble. He slammed it with the heel of his fist. It clattered into the vault, taking others with it. A dank scent of mildew gusted from the hole.

Eagerly, he clawed at the remaining bricks, pulling loose one then another, until the hole felt large enough for a man to squeeze through. Suddenly cautious, he paused. Cold rain trickled down his collar. Shivering, he struck another match. Sheltered in the hole, it kept its flame long enough for him to look in.

There was no coffin, just a heap of debris. For a miserable moment, he thought the vault had been empty. Then, even as the match was flickering out, he recognized a scattering of rotting wood and a few pieces of age-grayed bone in the debris.

The icy feeling of snakes squirmed along his spine again. But the image in his mind was a ruby bright as fire, burning away all thought, all fear. Dropping the matchstick, he wriggled through the opening he'd made.

Inside, he tried to sit up. His head hit the marble slab. Well, at least he was out of the rain, out of the wind. Propped on an elbow, he groped for the pieces of wood he'd seen. Identifying them by touch, he made a small pile of them, then struck his final match. The rotten wood was dry. It took flame readily, filling the vault with flickering light.

At last able to see what he was doing, Hull began scratching through the debris. Something round like a coin—but it was only a pewter button. He threw it on the fire. A piece of metal, evidently a coffin plate, was green with corrosion, the name eaten away. Another button. Bits of bone. A shred of rotted fabric. Broken pieces of brick. More wood.

He added the wood to his fire and continued his hunt.

Then there was no more wood and the fire was burning low. His fingers ached. He realized they were bleeding. And he'd found nothing.

The flame guttered out.

The darkness was not total. That puzzled Hull. Twisting, he turned himself within the narrow vault to face the entrance he'd made. Through it he could see a dim light. The moon had come out, he thought. That'd mean the icy rain was over. Moving closer, he peered through the hole.

The light was strange. Dim and misty, like a thin fog lying over the graveyard. There was no wind, only a silent stillness as unnatural as the light. Was it the stillness before a storm? he wondered. At least he had shelter inside the vault. Maybe he ought to stay the night there. No, he had to get hold of some money somewhere and get back the ruby.

The light was confusing. Nothing looked quite right. He thought he saw movement from the corner of an eye, but when he looked that way, there was only a tombstone.

Was it just a trick of the light? He hesitated, gazing out of the vault.

Another glimpsed motion, another tombstone.

Then he saw a furtive shape that darted from shadow to shadow.

He didn't believe in ghosts. Hell, no! It had to be something else. A grave-robber, he decided. Slowly, he grinned. The robber ought to know what grave was worth looking into. Let the robber do the work, then take his loot from him. That'd be easier than busting open vaults himself until he found the right one.

Wait! There was more than one of them.

His grin faded. More than one, more than two. It began to look as if someone was hidden in every shadow, behind every tombstone. A whole damned army of them.

Was the one he'd just glimpsed wearing a kepi? Was that a musket in the hand of the one disappearing behind a tombstone?

Oh Lord, he thought, could it be the Rebs hadn't evacuated the city? Had they just hid out? Were they massing here now to take Sherman's men by surprise? What if they found him? One lone Yankee without even his musket. What chance would he have?

His eyes seemed to be adjusting to the weird light. He could see a group of them in the shadow of a live oak. Vague shapes, shadows within a shadow. One leaning on a musket. No, not a musket. It was a crutch. Another with a bandaged head. Another with a crutch. Another in bandages.

They were coming out of the shadows, and he could see more bandages. Tattered clothes. Limping figures supported by their companions.

He sighed with relief. Not an attacking army, but walking wounded. Lame and halt, moving slowly, coming closer to where he lay hidden.

Then he saw the smallness of them. Not a man of them looked full grown. He frowned in puzzlement. A whole troop of drummer boys wounded in battle? Closer yet, and he saw more were too small even for drummers. And drummer boys didn't wear bonnets. Yes, there were girls among them, in ragged skirts, some with bandaged heads or arms or leaning on crutches like the boys. Some missing arms or legs or—God help him—was that one without a head?

They came on, and he could see their faces. White faces, and black faces, and every shade between. Round faces and gaunt faces. Hollow cheeks and hollow eyes. Eyes that gazed into the darkness, seeing into the darkness, into the vault. Staring at him where he lay. Staring at the tomb he had desecrated.

Suddenly he understood. Not from within himself. There was nothing within him capable of such understanding. It was as if they were putting it into his mind, silently, wordlessly, giving him comprehension.

They were the Third Nation—neither Union nor Confederate. The ones too young to have a say in the choosing of sides and the making of war. The ones brought into life and torn from it by acts not their own. Lives unfulfilled, bled away by shot and shell, seared away by untreated fevers and in burning buildings, shriveled by hunger and disease.

The lost children. The murdered children.

She stepped forward, a scrawny, dirty-faced towhead, her filthy rumpled dress flounced with tattered lace and holes in stockings that looked like silk.

He tried to speak, to beg, to tell her he was sorry; he'd really wanted to go back and let her out of the cupboard. But his throat was like ice and his breath a knot in his chest.

She took another step toward him.

He shrunk back into the vault. On his belly. Squirming away from her. Until he was against the wall and could go no farther.

He could no longer see her face, or anything else except the entrance hole he'd made into the vault. He could see only the light beyond the hole, the strange thin light like a luminous fog lying against the ragged opening.

Suddenly darkness bit a chunk from the rough circle of light. Then another. And another.

He realized they were replacing the bricks. Sealing the hole. And he knew, without even trying, that this time the mortar would not crumble under his knife.

THE GIRL WITH THE HUNGRY EYES

Fritz Leiber

All right, I'll tell you why the Girl gives me the creeps. Why I can't stand to go down town and see the mob slavering up at her on the tower, with that pop bottle or pack of cigarettes or whatever it is beside her. Why I hate to look at magazines anymore because I know she'll turn up somewhere in a brassiere or a bubble bath. Why I don't like to think of millions of Americans drinking in that poisonous half-smile. It's quite a story—more story than you're expecting.

No, I haven't suddenly developed any long-haired indignation at the evils of advertising and the national glamor-girl complex. That'd be a laugh for a man in my racket, wouldn't it? Though I think you'll agree there's something a little perverted about trying to capitalize on sex that way. But it's okay with me. And I know we've had the Face and the Body and the Look and what not else, so why shouldn't someone come along who sums it all up so completely, that we have to call her the Girl and blazon her on all the billboards from Times Square to Telegraph Hill?

But the Girl isn't like any of the others. She's unnatural. She's morbid. She's unholy.

Oh, these are modern times, you say, and the sort of thing I'm hinting at went out with witchcraft. But you see I'm not altogether sure myself what I'm hinting at, beyond a certain point. There are vampires and vampires, and not all of them suck blood.

And there were the murders, if they were murders. Besides, let me ask you this. Why, when America is obsessed with the Girl, don't we find out more about her? Why doesn't she rate a *Time* cover with a droll biography inside? Why hasn't there been a feature in *Life* or *The Post*? A profile in *The New Yorker*? Why hasn't *Charm* or *Mademoiselle* done her career saga? Not ready for it? Nuts!

Why haven't the movies snapped her up? Why hasn't she been on "Information, Please"? Why don't we see her kissing candidates at political rallies? Why isn't she chosen queen of some sort of junk or other at a convention?

Why don't we read about her tastes and hobbies, her views of the Russian situation? Why haven't the columnists interviewed her in a kimono on the top floor of the tallest hotel in Manhattan and told us who her boy friends are?

Finally—and this is the real killer—why hasn't she ever been drawn or painted?

Oh, no she hasn't. If you knew anything about commercial art you'd know that. Every blessed one of those pictures was worked up from a photograph. Expertly? Of course. They've got the top artists on it. But that's how it's done.

And now I'll tell you the why of all that. It's because from the top to the bottom of the whole world of advertising, news, and business, there isn't a solitary soul who knows where the Girl came from, where she lives, what she does, who she is, even what her name is.

You heard me. What's more, not a single solitary soul ever sees her—except one poor, damned photographer, who's making more money off her than he ever hoped to in his life and who's scared and miserable as Hell every minute of the day.

No, I haven't the faintest idea who he is or where he has his studio. But I know there has to be such a man and I'm morally certain he feels just like I said.

Yes, I might be able to find her, if I tried. I'm not sure though—by now she probably has other safeguards. Besides, I don't want to.

Oh, I'm off my rocker, am I? That sort of thing can't happen in the Era of the Atom? People can't keep out of sight that way, not even Garbo?

Well I happen to know they can, because last year I was that poor damned photographer I was telling you about. Yes, last year, when the Girl made her first poisonous splash right here in this big little city of ours.

Yes, I know you weren't here last year and you don't know about it. Even the Girl had to start small. But if you hunted through the files of the local newspapers, you'd find some ads, and I might be able to locate you some of the old displays—I think Lovelybelt is still using one of them. I used to have a mountain of photos myself, until I burned them.

Yes, I made my cut off her. Nothing like what that other photographer must be making, but enough so it still bought this whisky. She was funny about money. I'll tell you about that.

But first picture me then. I had a fourth-floor studio in that rathole the Hauser Building, not far from Ardleigh Park.

I'd been working at the Marsh-Mason studios until I'd gotten my bellyful of it and decided to start in for myself. The Hauser building was awful—I'll never forget how the stairs creaked—but it was cheap and there was a skylight.

Business was lousy. I kept making the rounds of all the advertisers and agencies, and some of them didn't object to me too much personally, but my stuff never clicked. I was pretty near broke. I was behind on my rent. Hell, I didn't even have enough money to have a girl.

It was one of those dark, gray afternoons. The building was very quiet—I'd just finished developing some pix I was doing on speculation for Lovelybelt Girdles and Budford's Pool and Playground. My model had left. A Miss Leon. She was a civics teacher at one of the high schools and modeled for me on the side, just lately on speculation, too. After one look at the prints, I decided that Miss Leon probably wasn't just what Lovelybelt was looking for—or my photography either. I was about to call it a day.

And then the street door slammed four stories down and there were steps on the stairs and she came in.

She was wearing a cheap, shiny black dress. Black pumps. No stockings. And except that she had a gray cloth coat over one of them, those skinny arms of hers were bare. Her arms are pretty skinny, you know, or can't you see things like that anymore?

And then the thin neck, the slightly gaunt, almost prim face, the tumbling mass of dark hair, and looking out from under it the hungriest eyes in the world.

That's the real reason she's plastered all over the country today, you know—those eyes. Nothing vulgar, but just the same they're looking at you with a hunger that's all sex and something more than sex. That's what everybody's been looking for since the Year One—something a little more than sex.

Well, boys, there I was, alone with the Girl, in an office that was getting shadowy, in a nearly empty building. A situation that a million male Americans have undoubtedly pictured to themselves with various lush details. How was I feeling? Scared.

I know sex can be frightening. That cold heart-thumping when you're alone with a girl and feel you're going to touch her. But if it was sex this time, it was overlaid with something else.

At least I wasn't thinking about sex.

I remember that I took a backward step and that my hand jerked so that the photos I was looking at sailed to the floor.

There was the faintest dizzy feeling like something was being drawn out of me just a little bit.

That was all. Then she opened her mouth and everything was back to normal for a while.

"I see you're a photographer, mister," she said. "Could you use a model?"

Her voice wasn't very cultivated.

"I doubt it," I told her, picking up the pix. You see, I

wasn't impressed. The commercial possibilities of her eyes hadn't registered on me yet, by a long shot. "What have you done?"

Well, she gave me a vague sort of story and I began to check her knowledge of model agencies and studios and rates and what not and pretty soon I said to her, "Look here, you never modeled for a photographer in your life. You just walked in here cold."

Well, she admitted that was more or less so.

All along through our talk I got the idea she was feeling her way, like someone in a strange place. Not that she was uncertain of herself, or of me, but just of the general situation.

"And you think anyone can model?" I asked her pityingly.

"Sure," she said.

"Look," I said, "a photographer can waste a dozen negatives trying to get one halfway human photo of an average woman. How many do you think he'd have to waste before he got a real catchy, glamorous photo of her?"

"I think I could do it," she said.

Well, I should have kicked her out right then. Maybe I admired the cool way she stuck to her dumb little guns. Maybe I was touched by her underfed look. More likely I was feeling mean on account of the way my pictures had been snubbed by everybody and I wanted to take it out on her by showing her up.

"Okay, I'm going to put you on the spot," I told her. "I'm going to try a couple of shots of you. Understand it's strictly on spec. If somebody should ever want to use a photo of you; which is about one chance in two million, I'll pay you regular rates for your time. Not otherwise."

She gave me a smile. The first. "That's swell by me," she said.

Well, I took three or four shots, close-ups of her face since I didn't fancy her cheap dress, and at least she stood up to my sarcasm. Then I remembered I still had the Lovelybelt stuff and I guess the meanness was still working in me because I handed her a girdle and told her to go behind the screen and get into it and she did, without getting flustered as I'd expected, and since we'd gone that far, I figured we might as well shoot the beach scene to round it out, and that was that.

All this time I wasn't feeling anything particular one way or the other, except every once in a while I'd get one of those faint dizzy flashes and wonder if there was something wrong with my stomach or if I could have been a bit careless with my chemicals.

Still, you know, I think the uneasiness was in me all the while.

I tossed her a card and pencil. "Write your name and address and phone," I told her and made for the darkroom.

A little later she walked out. I didn't call any good-byes. I was irked because she hadn't fussed around or seemed anxious about her poses, or even thanked me, except for that one smile.

I finished developing the negatives, made some prints, glanced at them, decided they weren't a great deal worse than Miss Leon. On an impulse I slipped them in with the pictures I was going to take on the rounds next morning.

By now I'd worked long enough, so I was a bit fagged and nervous, but I didn't dare waste enough money on liquor to help that. I wasn't very hungry. I think I went to a cheap movie.

I didn't think of the Girl at all, except maybe to wonder faintly why in my present womanless state I hadn't made a pass at her. She had seemed to belong to a—well, distinctly more approachable social strata than Miss Leon. But then, of course, there were all sorts of arguable reasons for my not doing that.

Next morning I made the rounds. My first step was Munsch's Brewery. They were looking for a "Munsch Girl." Papa Munsch had a sort of affection for me, though he razzed my photography. He had a good natural judgment about that, too. Fifty years ago he might have been one of the shoestring boys who made Hollywood.

Right now he was out in the plant pursuing his favorite occupation. He put down the beaded schooner, smacked his lips, gabbled something technical to someone about hops, wiped his hands on the big apron he was wearing, and grabbed my thin stack of pictures.

He was about halfway through, making noises with his tongue and teeth, when he came to her. I kicked myself for even having stuck her in.

"That's her," he said. "The photography's not so hot, but that's the girl."

It was all decided. I wonder now why Papa Munsch sensed what the Girl had right away, while I didn't. I think it was because I saw her first in the flesh, if that's the right word.

At the time I just felt faint.

"Who is she?" he said.

"One of my new models," I tried to make it casual.

"Bring her out tomorrow morning," he told me. "And your stuff. We'll photograph her here."

"Here, don't look so sick," he added. "Have some beer."

Well, I went away telling myself it was just a fluke, so that she'd probably blow it tomorrow with her inexperience, and so on.

Just the same, when I reverently laid my next stack of pictures on Mr. Fitch, of Lovelybelt's, rose-colored blotter, I had hers on top.

Mr. Fitch went through the motions of being an art critic. He leaned over backward, squinted his eyes, waved his long fingers, and said, "Hmm. What do you think, Miss Willow? Here, in this light, of course, the photograph doesn't show the bias cut. And perhaps we should use the Lovelybelt Imp instead of the Angel. Still, the girl . . . Come over here, Binns." More finger-waving. "I want a married man's reaction."

He couldn't hide the fact that he was hooked.

Exactly the same thing happened at Budford's Pool and Playground, except that Da Costa didn't need a married man's say-so.

"Hot stuff," he said, sucking his lips. "Oh boy, you photographers!"

I hotfooted it back to the office and grabbed up the card I'd given her to put down her name and address.

It was blank.

I don't mind telling you that the next five days were about the worst I ever went through, in an ordinary way. When next morning rolled around and I still hadn't got hold of her, I had to start stalling.

"She's sick," I told Papa Munsch over the phone.

"She at a hospital?" he asked me.

"Nothing that serious," I told him.

"Get her out here then. What's a little headache?"

"Sorry, I can't."

Papa Munsch got suspicious. "You really got this girl?"

"Of course I have."

"Well, I don't know. I'd think it was some New York model, except I recognized your lousy photography."

I laughed.

"Well look, you get her here tomorrow morning, you hear?"

"I'll try."

"Try nothing. You get her out here."

He didn't know half of what I tried. I went around to all the model and employment agencies. I did some slick detective work at the photographic and art studios. I used up some of my last dimes putting advertisements in all three papers. I looked at high school yearbooks and at employee photos in local house organs. I went to restaurants and drugstores, looking at waitresses, and to dime stores and department stores, looking at clerks. I watched the crowds coming out of movie theaters. I roamed the streets.

Evenings, I spent quite a bit of time along Pick-up Row. Somehow that seemed the right place.

The fifth afternoon I knew I was licked. Papa Munsch's deadline—he'd given me several, but this was it—was due to run out at six o'clock. Mr. Fitch had already canceled.

I was at the studio window, looking out at Ardleigh Park.

She walked in.

I'd gone over this moment so often in my mind that

I had no trouble putting on my act. Even the faint dizzy feeling didn't throw me off.

"Hello," I said, hardly looking at her.

"Hello," she said.

"Not discouraged yet?"

"No." It didn't sound uneasy or defiant. It was just a statement.

I snapped a look at my watch, got up, and said curtly, "Look here, I'm going to give you a chance. There's a client of mine looking for a girl your general type. If you do a real good job you might break into the modeling business."

"We can see him this afternoon if we hurry," I said. I picked up my stuff. "Come on. And next time if you expect favors, don't forget to leave your phone number."

"Uh, uh," she said, not moving.

"What do you mean?" I said.

"I'm not going out to see any client of yours."

"The hell you aren't," I said. "You little nut, I'm giving you a break."

She shook her head slowly. "You're not fooling me, baby, you're not fooling me at all. They want me." And she gave me the second smile.

At the time I thought she must have seen my newspaper ad. Now I'm not so sure.

"And now I'll tell you how we're going to work," she went on. "You aren't going to have my name or address or phone number. Nobody is. And we're going to do all the pictures right here. Just you and me."

You can imagine the roar I raised at that. I was everything—angry, sarcastic, patiently explanatory, off my nut, threatening, pleading.

I would have slapped her face off, except it was photographic capital.

In the end all I could do was phone Papa Munsch and tell him her conditions. I knew I didn't have a chance, but I had to take it.

He gave me a really angry bawling out, said "no" several times, and hung up.

It didn't worry her. "We'll start shooting at ten o'clock tomorrow," she said.

It was just like her, using that corny line from the movie magazines.

About midnight Papa Munsch called me up.

"I don't know what insane asylum you're renting this girl from," he said, "but I'll take her. Come round tomorrow morning and I'll try to get it through your head just how I want the pictures. And I'm glad I got you out of bed!"

After that it was a breeze. Even Mr. Fitch reconsidered and after taking two days to tell me it was quite impossible, he accepted the conditions too.

Of course you're all under the spell of the Girl, so you can't understand how much self-sacrifice it represented on Mr. Fitch's part when he agreed to forego supervising the photography of my model in the Lovelybelt Imp or Vixen or whatever it was we finally used.

Next morning she turned up on time according to her schedule, and we went to work. I'll say one thing for her, she never got tired and she never kicked at the way I fussed over shots. I got along okay, except I still had that feeling of something being shoved away gently. Maybe you've felt it just a little, looking at her picture.

When we finished I found out there were still more rules. It was about the middle of the afternoon. I started with her to get a sandwich and coffee.

"Uh, uh," she said, "I'm going down alone. And look, baby, if you ever try to follow me, if you ever so much as stick your head out of that window when I go, you can hire yourself another model."

You can imagine how all this crazy stuff strained my temper—and my imagination. I remember opening the window after she was gone—I waited a few minutes first—and standing there getting some fresh air and trying to figure out what could be behind it, whether she was hiding from the police, or was somebody's ruined daughter, or maybe had got the idea it was smart to be temperamental, or more likely Papa Munsch was right and she was partly nuts.

But I had my pictures to finish up.

Looking back it's amazing to think how fast her magic began to take hold of the city after that. Remembering what came after, I'm frightened of what's happening to the whole country—and maybe the world. Yesterday I read something in *Time* about the Girl's picture turning up on billboards in Egypt.

The rest of my story will help show you why I'm frightened in that big, general way. But I have a theory, too, that helps explain, though it's one of those things that's beyond that "certain point." It's about the Girl. I'll give it to you in a few words.

You know how modern advertising gets everybody's mind set in the same direction, wanting the same things, imagining the same things. And you know the psychologists aren't so skeptical of telepathy as they used to be.

Add up the two ideas. Suppose the identical desires of millions of people focused on one telepathic person. Say a girl. Shaped her in their image.

Imagine her knowing the hiddenmost hungers of millions of men. Imagine her seeing deeper into those hungers than the people that had them, seeing the hatred and the wish for death behind the lust. Imagine her shaping herself in that complete image, keeping herself as aloof as marble. Yet imagine the hunger she might feel in answer to their hunger.

But that's getting a long way from the facts of my story. And some of those facts are darn solid. Like money. We made money.

That was the funny thing I was going to tell you. I was afraid the Girl was going to hold me up. She really had me over a barrel, you know.

But she didn't ask for anything but the regular rates. Later on I insisted on pushing more money at her, a whole lot. But she always took it with that same contemptuous look, as if she were going to toss it down the first drain when she got outside.

Maybe she did.

At any rate, I had money. For the first time in months I had money enough to get drunk, buy new clothes, take taxicabs. I could make a play for any girl I wanted to. I only had to pick.

And so of course I had to go and pick . . .

But first let me tell you about Papa Munsch.

Papa Munsch wasn't the first of the boys to try to meet my model but I think he was the first to really go soft on her. I could watch the change in his eyes as he looked at her pictures. They began to get sentimental, reverent. Mama Munsch had been dead for two years.

He was smart about the way he planned it. He got me to drop some information which told him when she came to work, and then one morning he came pounding up the stairs a few minutes before.

"I've got to see her, Dave," he told me.

I argued with him, I kidded him, I explained he didn't know just how serious she was about her crazy ideas. I even pointed out he was cutting both our throats. I even amazed myself by bawling him out.

He didn't take any of it in his usual way. He just kept repeating, "But Dave, I've got to see her."

The street door slammed.

"That's her," I said, lowering my voice. "You've got to get out."

He wouldn't, so I shoved him in the darkroom. "And keep quiet," I whispered. "I'll tell her I can't work today."

I knew he'd try to look at her and probably come bustling in, but there wasn't anything else I could do.

The footsteps came to the fourth floor. But she never showed at the door. I got uneasy.

"Get the bum out of here!" she yelled suddenly from beyond the door. Not very loud, but in her commonest voice.

"I'm going up to the next landing," she said. "And if that fat-bellied bum doesn't march straight down to the street, he'll never get another picture of me except spitting in his lousy beer."

Papa Munsch came out of the darkroom. He was white. He didn't look at me as he went out. He never looked at her pictures in front of me again.

That was Papa Munsch. Now it's me I'm telling about. I talked around the subject with her, I hinted, eventually I made my pass.

She lifted my hand off her as if it were a damp rag.

"No, baby," she said. "This is working time."

"But afterward . . ." I pressed.

"The rules still hold." And I got what I think was the fifth smile.

It's hard to believe, but she never budged an inch from that crazy line. I mustn't make a pass at her in the office, because our work was very important and she loved it and there mustn't be any distractions. And I couldn't see her anywhere else, because if I tried to, I'd never snap another picture of her—and all this with more money coming in all the time and me never so stupid as to think my photography had anything to do with it.

Of course I wouldn't have been human if I hadn't made more passes. But they always got the wet-rag treatment and there weren't any more smiles.

I changed. I went sort of crazy and light-headed—only sometimes I felt my head was going to burst. And I started to talk to her all the time. About myself.

It was like being in a constant delirium that never interfered with business. I didn't pay any attention to the dizzy feeling. It seemed natural.

I'd walk around and for a moment the reflector would look like a sheet of white-hot steel, or the shadows would seem like armies of moths, or the camera would be a big black coal car. But the next instant they'd come all right again.

I think sometimes I was scared to death of her. She'd seem the strangest, most horrible person in the world. But other times . . .

And I talked. It didn't matter what I was doing—lighting her, posing her, fussing with props, snapping my pictures—or where she was—on the platform, behind the screen, relaxing with a magazine—I kept up a steady gab.

I told her everything I knew about myself. I told her about my first girl. I told her about my brother Bob's bicycle. I told her about running away on a freight, and the licking Pa gave me when I came home. I told her about shipping to South America and the blue sky at night. I told her about Betty. I told her about my mother dying of cancer. I told her about being beaten up in a fight in an alley behind a bar. I told her about Mildred. I told her about the first picture I ever sold. I told her how Chicago looked from a sailboat. I told her about the longest drunk I was ever on. I told her about Marsh-Mason. I told her about Gwen. I told her about how I met Papa Munsch. I told her about hunting her. I told her about how I felt now.

She never paid the slightest attention to what I said. I couldn't even tell if she heard me.

It was when we were getting our first nibble from national advertisers that I decided to follow her when she went home.

Wait, I can place it better than that. Something you'll remember from the out-of-town papers—those maybe murders I mentioned. I think there were six.

I say "maybe" because the police could never be sure they weren't heart attacks. But there's bound to be suspicion when attacks happen to people whose hearts have been okay, and always at night when they're alone and away from home and there's a question of what they were doing.

The six deaths created one of those "mystery poisoner" scares. And afterward there was a feeling that they hadn't really stopped, but were being continued in a less suspicious way.

That's one of the things that scares me now.

But at that time my only feeling was relief that I'd decided to follow her.

I made her work until dark one afternoon. I didn't need any excuses, we were snowed under with orders. I waited until the street door slammed, then I ran down. I was wearing rubber-soled shoes. I'd slipped on a dark coat she'd never seen me in, and a dark hat.

I stood in the doorway until I spotted her. She was walking by Ardleigh Park toward the heart of town. It was one of those warm fall nights. I followed her on the other side of the street. My idea for tonight was just to find out where she lived. That would give me a hold on her.

She stopped in front of a display window of Everley's department store, standing back from the flow. She stood there looking in.

I remembered we'd done a big photograph of her for Everley's, to make a flat model for a lingerie display. That was what she was looking at.

At the time it seemed all right to me that she should adore herself, if that was what she was doing.

When people passed she'd turn away a little or drift back farther into the shadows.

Then a man came by alone. I couldn't see his face very well, but he looked middle-aged. He stopped and stood looking in the window.

She came out of the shadows and stepped up beside him.

How would you boys feel if you were looking at a poster of the Girl and suddenly she was there beside you, her arm linked with yours?

This fellow's reaction showed plain as day. A crazy dream had come to life for him.

They talked for a moment. Then he waved a taxi to the curb. They got in and drove off.

I got drunk that night. It was almost as if she'd known I was following her and had picked that way to hurt me. Maybe she had. Maybe this was the finish.

But the next morning she turned up at the usual time and I was back in the delirium, only now with some new angles added.

That night when I followed her she picked a spot under a street lamp, opposite one of the Munsch Girl billboards.

Now it frightens me to think of her lurking that way.

After about twenty minutes a convertible slowed down going past her, backed up, swung into the curb.

I was closer this time. I got a good look at the fellow's face. He was a little younger, about my age.

Next morning the same face looked up at me from the front page of the paper. The convertible had been found parked on a side street. He had been in it. As in the other maybe-murders, the cause of death was uncertain.

All kinds of thoughts were spinning in my head that day, but there were only two things I knew for sure. That I'd got the first real offer from a national advertiser, and that I was going to take the Girl's arm and walk down the stairs with her when we quit work.

She didn't seem surprised. "You know what you're doing?" she said.

"I know."

She smiled. "I was wondering when you'd get around to it."

I began to feel good. I was kissing everything good-bye, but I had my arm around hers.

It was another of those warm fall evenings. We cut across into Ardleigh Park. It was dark there, but all around the sky was a sallow pink from the advertising signs.

We walked for a long time in the park. She didn't say anything and she didn't look at me, but I could see her lips twitching and after a while her hand tightened on my arm.

We stopped. We'd been walking across the grass. She dropped down and pulled me after her. She put her hands on my shoulders. I was looking down at her face. It was the faintest sallow pink from the glow in the sky. The hungry eyes were dark smudges.

I was fumbling with her blouse. She took my hand away, not like she had in the studio. "I don't want that," she said.

FIRST I'LL TELL YOU what I did afterward. Then I'll tell you why I did it. Then I'll tell you what she said.

What I did was run away. I don't remember all of that because I was dizzy, and the pink sky was swinging against the dark trees. But after a while I staggered into the lights of the street. The next day I closed up the studio. The telephone was ringing when I locked the door and there were unopened letters on the floor. I never saw the Girl again in the flesh, if that's the right word.

I did it because I didn't want to die. I didn't want the life drawn out of me. There are vampires and vampires, and the ones that suck blood aren't the worst. If it hadn't been for the warning of those dizzy flashes, and Papa Munsch and the face in the morning paper, I'd have gone the way the others did. But I realized what I was up against while there was still time to tear myself away. I realized that wherever she came from, whatever shaped her, she's the quintessence of the horror behind the bright billboard. She's the smile that tricks you into throwing away your money and your life. She's the eyes that lead you on and on, and then show you death. She's the creature you give everything for and never really get. She's the being that takes everything you've got and gives nothing in return. When you yearn toward her face on the billboards, remember that. She's the lure. She's the bait. She's the Girl.

And this is what she said, "I want you. I want your high spots. I want everything that's made you happy and everything that's hurt you bad. I want your first girl. I want that shiny bicycle. I want that licking. I want that pinhole camera. I want Betty's legs. I want the blue sky filled with stars. I want your mother's death. I want your blood on the cobblestones. I want Mildred's mouth. I want the first picture you sold. I want the lights of Chicago. I want the gin. I want Gwen's hands. I want your wanting me. I want your life. Feed me, baby, feed me."

FOOD CHAIN

Nina Kiriki Hoffman

Cissy told me Saturday night that she needed a new mother, so Sunday morning I started the coffeemaker, then woke the others a little before they normally got up. We gathered in Dark House's roomy kitchen.

"What is it this time, Alice?" Francesca said, sprawling at the big round table, her dark eyes heavy lidded and her thick black hair in snarls. I undimmed the overhead light, making it bright enough to read recipes. The kitchen was at the back of the house and didn't get any sunlight until evening. Francesca winced and covered her eyes. She was a chef at the three-star restaurant around the corner from Dark House, and she worked every night except Saturday, when she prowled in search of adventure. Sunday was the worst morning of her week.

145

Dora got spinach and bacon out of the refrigerator. She always woke up faster than the rest of us, even in summer when she wasn't teaching grade school. She switched on a burner and set a skillet on it. "C'mon," she said, shaking Micki's shoulder. "Wash." She pointed at the spinach by the sink. Micki sat for a moment with her broad shoulders hunched and her eyes closed, probably hoping the job would go away if she ignored it. Then she stood and ambled over to the sink.

Bettina put a full kettle of water on for tea and brought the assortment of things-hot-water-instantly-created to the table so the rest of us could pick through the packets. "What's up?" she said. Her English accent was crisp. Her voice reminded me of BBC radio news. I liked listening to her. "You should be in bed, Alice. It's your morning after."

I did feel tired. I got myself a big glass of orange juice and two chocolate-glazed doughnuts. "We need another mother," I said.

"That's ridiculous," said Zelda. I sipped orange juice and looked at her over the rim of my glass. She had just gotten a new haircut, one quite popular when I was a girl, but in those days crew cuts were only seen on boys. Her blonde stubble glistened as she tilted her head back, the better to stare down her nose at me.

"Coffee?" Gail asked, smothering a yawn with the back of her hand. She was wearing a short silky green nightgown and nothing else. It had taken me some time to accustom myself to her informality. Things were different when I was young. My parents never pranced around the house in next to nothing; if they left their bedroom, they always wore robes, and so had my husband and I when we became parents.

Zelda, Micki, and Dora said yes to coffee. Gail got down four mugs, filled them, and brought them to the table.

"Cissy told me we need another mother," I said.

"Why?" Zelda said. Her blue eyes narrowed as she stared at me. "There's seven of us. That's enough."

I put down my glass. I studied my hands, touched the fingers of the left with the fingers of my right. Skin that had once been smooth, taut with muscle and life, was papery now, pleated. When I pressed it sideways it did not spring back immediately. I felt a monumental tiredness in me. I was always tired the morning after my night with Cissy; we all were. But it had never felt so sapping before; usually it was a pleasant languor, an excuse to linger in bed and eat special foods.

"Oh, Alice," Gail said, putting down her mug and coming around the table to stoop beside me and hug me. Her warmth and her kindness and energy penetrated me as though I were gauze in the path of sunlight, and I lost my frail hold on control. Tears started down my face.

"Alice," Bettina murmured, her voice gentle.

"I'm sorry," I said. Micki came and stroked her big hand down my back, tracing the leaves of elephant clovers there. For a long while, no one else said anything. The only sounds were the sizzle and pop of bacon on the stove, and my breath catching on itself. The fragrance of brewing coffee and frying bacon reminded me of countless breakfasts stretching backward through time, some just the pleasant beginnings to indifferent days, some interrupted by news—Daddy was not coming back from the war (Mother dropped the frypan when she heard, and grease spatters from the bacon burned her legs); my sister Lucy had delivered a boy (a moment of silence, thanks to God); my own precious little daughter Johanna had not survived the night (but that had been a morning smelling of disinfectant and cigarette smoke, in a dingy hospital waiting room, because the doctors did not trust me in the room with my own child, so that I missed her last moments, missed holding her hand until God could take it from me).

I remembered how time had stretched in those moments, how during the bad ones I had thought the pain would never lessen, that I would live in an eternal Now of hurt that tears would not be able to wash away.

But in this Now, I was with those I loved, and no one was dying. Moments moved inexorably from Now to next, and carried me away from my own sorrow. I got myself back under control, patted Gail's head, blotted my tears on a paper napkin, sipped my quiet sobs away with orange juice.

"How long have you been here, Alice?" asked Francesca, wide awake now.

"Thirty-seven years."

Dora set her spinach salad in the center of the table and handed bowls and forks around.

"How old were you when you got here?" Francesca said.

"Twenty-six."

Zelda put her hand over mine. "What happened," she said, "to the other mothers? The ones we replaced?"

"I don't know." The population of Dark House shifted; sometimes people came for a while and left; sometimes there were ten of us and our nights with Cissy were farther between; I knew that others had grown old here, but I could not remember who they had been or where they had gone. I had the feeling that there was only one Cissy, though; despite what the movies and the books said about people like Cissy, what she had wasn't a disease that turned people who came in contact with her into people like her. But then, movies and books were wrong about all sorts of things.

"I'm so afraid of leaving," I said, and hid my eyes behind my hand.

Zelda's hand was warm on mine. Her thumb stroked along the curve formed by my thumb and forefinger. "Is that what happens?" she murmured. "Do people have to leave?"

"I don't know," I said. "My memory is . . ."

"Cissified," said Micki. She had been at Dark House for seventeen years, and everyone else for less time.

"What?" asked Bettina. She was our newest mother.

"Remember when you decided to come here?" Micki said.

"Of course—I was standing at the fence outside the preschool where Gareth used to go, watching the children, and—no, I didn't know about you or the house then, I just had that overpowering feeling that there was nothing, nothing on Earth left for me to do, that every day would be gray and stars would never shine again. And then . . ."

"Then," said Zelda, "I woke up. I was lying on a soft bed in a strange room I had never seen before, and little Benjamin was lying next to me. I hugged him and told him never ever to leave me again. And he said he wouldn't. Or at least that I could see him once a week."

Her gaze was fixed on a copper-bottomed pan hanging on the wall, and her voice sounded light and far away, as if she were describing a dream while she was still asleep. "How could that be? At his funeral I touched his face, I had to, because I kept thinking he wasn't really dead, he couldn't be dead, he was only two years old, such a perfect little being, and I would lie awake listening and listening for him to cry again so I could go comfort him. I touched his face and it was cold and stiff and I knew he was gone and Robert hugged me and took me away but even though I knew Benjamin was gone, I still couldn't let go of him and somehow Robert couldn't take it after awhile, and . . . and then I woke up, and there he was, my baby."

I gripped Zelda's hand. After a moment she blinked and looked at me and smiled.

Bettina looked at Micki.

"It's like that for all of us. Cissy can do something to the memories," Micki said. "I know everything I need to know about nursing, and about everyone on staff at the hospital, and I know my brother's phone number— I talk to him every week. I remember my childhood, my marriage, the birth of my child and her every word or act. I even remember her death. And then . . . there's a fuzzy period. I think I went crazy. I really think I must have. I got stuck. I stayed in the house and didn't wash or eat. I was waiting for little Annie to come back. The life was leaking out of me. My husband tried everything to rouse me out of it, but he couldn't.

"Then I woke up," Micki said. She smiled, looking inward. Her big arms curled into a cradle.

"Yes," said Dora. She had dished out salad for everybody and passed it around, but no one was tasting it. "Micki and I have been comparing memories. Cissy can manipulate them, apparently. I don't feel like a different person. I don't feel controlled. I'm here because I want to be. Still, there are some things in my head I can't seem to get to."

An image of my own hands bleeding and hurt flashed through my mind. I remembered. I remembered hammering fists against the beige hospital walls of that waiting room until I left bloody marks. I remembered my own mother trying to catch my wrists and stop me, telling me my behavior was unladylike and undignified, as if I had dropped a spoon at afternoon tea. I remembered the rage rising in me like a great smothering wave.

I blinked and the memory vanished. I was glad it was gone.

"I remember Carol and Debbie," said Micki, and as she said the names, pictures of the women came into my head. Carol had been thin and remote, and it seemed to me she came and stayed just a little while and left. Left! I remembered her packing. I remembered touching her hand in farewell, and thinking it felt cold. Debbie had been large, and friendly on the surface, but I had never found myself telling her anything important, not after I told her about the secret party to celebrate Micki's promotion to head nurse of her floor, and Debbie told Micki.

Zelda was prickly and irritable, and Francesca was lazy. There were things about each of the others that annoyed me in small ways, but I felt I could tell them anything and they would not betray me.

Micki said, "Dora and I have been trying to fish up the names of others. Alice . . ."

"I didn't remember until you said them, Micki," I said. "Now I do, and I don't see how that helps. I'm glad they didn't stay."

"The real question is," said Micki, "how did Cissy find us? I can't remember meeting her before waking up in bed with her. If we're going to find another mother— how?"

GAIL COOKED SUNDAY NIGHTS. She was the youngest mother in Dark House and had grown up in an age that no longer demanded that its women know how to cook. Francesca had bought her a basic cookbook, and we all helped on occasion. Gail had been in the house four years and no longer lamented the loss of microwaves; Cissy said they disturbed her sleep.

That night she made some kind of Hungarian stew with a lot of spices and chunks of vegetables in a big pot. She had dropped a piece of potato on the burner and the kitchen had that after-an-accident tang in the air. The stew, besides being burnt, was a little strong for me, and I only ate a little, filling up on crusty bakery French bread instead. I was sipping heavily creamed coffee and watching the others (except for Francesca, who worked from four to nine Sunday evenings) struggle to say something nice about the food, or even to finish it, when Cissy came yawning up from the basement.

I didn't know how the others dealt with Cissy's changes. I made two places for her in my mind: Cissy-in-common, a slight, colorless girl of eleven or so, whom no one would have noticed until she smiled—something of her smile was so sweet and sad it burned like raw sugar on the tongue; and Cissy-in-private, whom I called Johanna, and whom the others called by the names of their own departed children. My relationship with Cissy-in-common was very different from my relationship with Cissy-in-private.

"Hi, kiddo," Gail said, waving a fork with a piece of potato on it.

Cissy flapped a hand in front of her face. "Phew! Paprika city!"

"You don't like paprika?" Gail asked, stricken. There were some spices and condiments we had to be careful with. I remembered, suddenly, taking Micki shopping when she first came to Dark House, nixing the garlic powder: "It gets in the milk. Not good for the baby," I had said, and Micki had accepted that without question.

"It's not my favorite," Cissy said. "It's not so bad, though." She smiled.

"So," said Zelda, laying her spoon across an edge of her bowl, "another mother, Cissy? Alice said another mother."

Cissy sat down beside me. She looked breakable. I gripped my left hand in my right. When had it happened? When had I become too old to give her what she needed?

Her small cold hand closed around my wrist and she looked up into my eyes. For a moment I saw my Johanna, her eyes like wet violets, her cheeks pink as sunrise, downy dark hair lying flat on her head no matter how I tried to tease it into curling. A rush of love, hot and red and all embracing, rose in me. I knew that what I lived for, what satisfied me most of anything on this Earth, was to care for this child, this seed of a plant not yet known, this vessel of all potentials; that the best thing I could ever do was to nurture my little one and take joy in everything she did. I knew this in my mind and in my heart and in that place deep within me that connected me to every mother who had ever lived. My breasts felt warm and full and ready; my eyelids felt too heavy to keep open.

"Alice," Cissy murmured, her small chill hand tugging at mine, pulling my right hand away from my left. "Alice."

I jerked awake again, looked down at her pale, worried face.

"I didn't—" she said. "I didn't mean—"

An arrow of heat touched my left eye and a tear spilled out of it. Sunday wasn't my night. Sunday was Zelda's night. Anyway, Cissy never spent two nights in a row with anyone. Especially not someone who didn't have anything to give her, I thought, looking down at my sagging breasts. Here in Dark House, age had crept up on me while I wasn't watching. It had shocked me when they suggested at the library that it was time for me to retire. I had always felt fine.

I glanced up at Zelda, who for once didn't look supercilious, only sad. Perhaps she had seen love and desire naked on my face in a way that I had never seen it on any of the others'. Today was the first time I had spoken with the others about what Cissy really did for each of us. I had known, the way I had known as a young woman that every woman must menstruate, but I had not let myself know; I had blanked my mind. One night a week I had with Cissy, bright as the sun, and the other nights I went to sleep alone, that was all there was to it.

"Cissy," said Dora after a moment. "We've been trying to remember how we got here, and we can't. We don't know how you recruit mothers."

Cissy patted my hand and then stopped touching me. "Do you need to know?" she asked.

"Alice told us you want somebody new."

"I will find her," said Cissy.

"What happens to those who are too old?" Bettina asked. My mother's voice rose in my memory, telling me that that was an unladylike question, though said in such a lovely tone of voice. One shouldn't speak of such things.

"Do you need to know?" Cissy said.

There was a brief silence. Micki said, "I would like to know. I'm the eldest after Alice. I imagine I'll grow old here in Dark House, as she has. I think Alice might like to know what comes next. I realize you can tell us and then take this memory away from us as you have with other memories. So why not tell us? And what happened to the people who didn't work out?"

Cissy frowned. She stared at the tabletop with furrowed brows.

"Come on, Cissy. What harm could it do?" Micki sounded like a hearty nurse telling you it was time for your shot, but it wouldn't hurt, no matter how often you'd had a hurting shot before.

"I've never told anyone."

"Aw, c'mon, kiddo," said Gail. "Not anybody? In however long you've been at this? Didn't you ever want to?"

"Is what you do so terrible?" Dora asked.

Cissy looked up, meeting each of our gazes in turn. "Everything I do is terrible," she said in a small frozen voice.

"It is not," said Zelda, in the tone one uses to reassure one's child of how special it is, even though it has just made a mistake.

"You do not know what I do," said Cissy, almost whispering, "or what I have done in the past."

I wanted to gather her into my arms and hug her into silence. I wanted to just think about her as the perfect little child who was not old enough to be responsible for its actions, whose only reason for existing was to be loved, and whom I could love in a way that made me a perfect mother. I put my hand on her shoulder. She felt cold, and her shoulder was very small.

Dora said, "We can't know, unless you tell us, Cissy. You can tell us, and then you can untell us, if you like."

Cissy put her hands over her face.

"I don't want to know," I said, surprising myself. "If it hurts you to tell us, I don't want to know."

For a moment no one said anything. Then Cissy's voice came out from between her hands. "The ones who come, the ones who do not stay, I take their memories away and give them a very strong urge to go far away from here and never to speak about it."

"What's so terrible about that?" asked Gail.

Cissy lowered her hands, wove her fingers through each other and gripped hard.

"Those of you who stay," she said, and stopped.

Bettina sipped tea. The click of her cup on her saucer was the only sound.

Cissy spoke to her hands. "You give me what I need. You give, and I take."

"You give us what we need too," Micki said after a long moment.

Cissy shook her head.

Micki cleared her throat, then said, "I would have died."

"No."

Micki, big, solid, practical Micki, said, "I would have died, Cissy."

Cissy closed her eyes and shook her head. "No," she said. "No. You can't even remember that."

"I can. I do. I would have died without you, Cissy. You gave me what I needed."

"I gave you a lie!"

Bettina gasped. Her arms came up, crossed at the wrists, to cover her breasts, as though she had suddenly realized she was nude.

"Sometimes we need lies to survive," Dora said.

Cissy looked up. Her eyes were dark. "I'm a parasite."

"We all live off life, one way or another," said Zelda. "We kill what we eat right away, and you don't."

Cissy licked her lips. Even her tongue was pale. She must, I thought, be very hungry. "Tonight, after I feed," she said, "I will go out and taste the air, searching for a particular flavor of despair. I will follow it to its source, and I will take that source away from everything she has ever known and bring her here."

And I remembered where I had been when I first saw Cissy. Lying in a bed with bars on it, with straps buckled around my wrists and ankles, and all my hair shaved off. Lying in my own urine because the orderly didn't like me; I reminded him of his mother, he had said, and I had screamed. I had still been screaming, off and on, when Cissy called to me through the bars on the window, asking if she could come in. I had screamed yes. And she came and lay on my breast and I had my Johanna back again; and I could let go of my screams.

"You took me away from my despair and gave me back a life," I said.

THAT NIGHT I COULD not sleep. I went down to the kitchen and fixed warm milk with honey, the same potion my mother had brewed for me when I was a little girl and the night seemed full of monsters. I took my mug back up to my room and sat reading in bed, pillows behind me, my wedding ring quilt lapping at my waist. My gaze wandered across the words in my book without fastening on any of them. I stared and stared, trying to drop down into the story the way I usually did, but it was no use.

I put the book away and sat thinking about being a children's librarian, how I had loved to watch the little ones discover words and pictures, as Johanna might have, if she had lived longer, how there were almost always one or two who read deeply and wanted the new and bright and best, how their ever-fresh excitement made my job new and worthwhile, even though there were others who drew on the pages or tore them or lost books. Johanna would never grow older, but other children did; with Cissy in my arms I could dream, a different dream every week, each better than the last, and all of them equally likely to come true.

I no longer had the library, though I went there and did a weekly story hour. The new librarian didn't care for it when I stayed. The children liked me better and came to me with questions.

The library no longer gave me purpose, and Cissy could no longer give me purpose. I didn't think I could stay in Dark House, seeing her every evening but not being able to spend my special time with her. I could not think of anywhere else on Earth to go. The friends of my marriage had dropped away when I went into the mental hospital, and somehow, with so many friends at home, I had not pursued relationships outside of Dark House.

My mother was dead, and I had no idea whether my husband was alive.

I was staring beyond the circle of my lamp, trying without success to see the painting across the room (though I had memorized it during the daylight hours, with only a faint illumination it appeared a different picture altogether, more sinister) when the door eased open and Cissy came in, white as any angel and silent as a cloud.

Her cheeks bloomed with the transient health I had once been able to give her; her eyes sparkled. She looked more alive than most of the children I saw in the street. She came to me and climbed up on the bed, sitting nightgowned and barefoot facing me.

"Alice," she said, holding out her hand. I took it and felt the rosy warmth of her fingers.

"What is it?" I said. My throat felt tight.

"I have something to give you," she said. Her words were pregnant with joy and mystery.

My throat closed tighter still. "Cissy, I don't know what to do," I whispered.

"You don't have to know. You don't have to know anything. Close your eyes."

I closed my eyes and felt the tears gathering in my chest and in my throat. Sadness was a swamp; the mire enclosed me and I did not know how to pull free of it.

And then I felt arms come around me, gathering me close into a warm embrace. A breast pillowed my head. I pulled my knees up close to my chest and knew that somehow, someone held me in her lap.

I opened my eyes just a little and the face I saw above mine was not my mother's, but someone's mother, the mother I had always wished I had had. Her smile was gentle, her eyes tender. "You are my special child," she whispered, "the child of all my dreams, and I love you."

She fed me the milk of contentment. There was no longer anything I wanted or could even think of wanting, and so at last I let go of all my desires.

THE MAGIC-STEALER

Josepha Sherman

Nitika staggered to a stop, all at once painfully aware of weariness and cold. Shivering, she glanced around, one slim, black-haired girl of sixteen years. The forest was a lonely place in the fading orange light of afternoon, barren with the coming of winter. Empty branches creaked and scraped together in the chill gusts of wind, and the air was sharp with the promise of snow.

A new bout of shivering tore through her. Nitika clutched the folds of her deerskin robe more tightly about herself, wishing it were fur.

Skanea had never needed fur, whispered her mind, not she, who could warm herself with a simple flash of will.

Skanea, who was dead . . .

Suddenly the forest seemed to blur. *I will not weep!* the girl told herself fiercely, wiping a hand roughly across her eyes. The necklaces she wore chinked together softly, and Nitika winced in new pain. These were a Power-Speaker's necklaces, full of magic, charms of bone and shell and wood:

Skanea's necklaces left to Nitika, her apprentice in Power.

Apprentice. No more than that.

A true Power-Speaker, a magician-healer like Skanea, could calm the winter wind, or walk through a blizzard and not feel the slightest cold. Nitika *had* managed to ward off the chill for a time. But as always, the force of her will had faded, and the Power with it.

"You were wrong," she whispered to Skanea's spirit. "I'm no Power-Speaker. I never will be."

But what else was there for her? Though none of the People had ever been anything but kind to her, Nitika, orphaned almost from birth, with only distant clan relations to care for her, had had no real place in any of the lodges. But old Skanea, then Power-Speaker for the tribe, had quickly taken the frightened child under her wing as apprentice.

Nitika smiled fleetingly, remembering those early days. At first it had been wonderful, learning the smallest bits of Power, dreaming of the day when she, too, could walk with spirits and work true magic.

But then, when she was nearly ten, the trouble had come, in the form of Gungosah, a man of the People just returned from long journeyings: proud, ambitious Gungosah, who also claimed Power for himself. He and Skanea had quarreled bitterly. To the old woman's disgust, the People had favored Gungosah; he was young and handsome, while Skanea was rough of tongue and face. Besides, what tribe needed two Power-Speakers? Skanea had gone storming off into the wilderness to live. And, though it had hurt to leave home and playmates, Nitika had gone with her.

Nitika sighed, her breath a plume on the frosty air. It had been lonely sometimes, with just the two of them and sometimes the funny or dangerous little spirits of the wood. Skanea had promised her that once her apprenticeship was done, they would return to the People.

But that apprenticeship could never end now. For in the midst of Nitika's final tests of Power, Skanea's heart had given out. Her dying words lingered in the girl's mind:

"Take my necklaces. You are Power-Speaker in all but name. You are! Believe!"

Nitika hid her face in her hands. *How can I believe?* she asked Skanea's spirit silently. *Without my final testing, no spell will work for me.*

If she stayed out here without shelter, she'd freeze. She would return to the lodges of the People. There was nowhere else. Head down, Nitika started wearily forward.

Just then, a male voice asked doubtfully, "Nitika . . . ?"

She looked up with a gasp. A young man in a hunter's tunic and leggings—a boy, really, perhaps a little older than herself—stood before her, a bow slung over his shoulder, staring at her as though she was the most wonderful thing he had ever seen. He was tall and slender, with the high cheekbones and dark reddish skin of the People; and, thought Nitika, he was handsome, too. Even if his nose was just a tiny bit crooked . . .

A sudden warm memory flashed into her mind of a little boy with a slightly crooked nose and bright, laughing eyes: Tehanyah, her dearest childhood friend. They had played together so happily in the long-ago days. Before Skanea had taken her away from the People. "Tehanyah? But you've grown so—so—" Her tongue stumbled over the word "handsome" "—so tall!"

"And you've grown so pretty," Tehanyah burst out, then dropped his gaze in embarrassment, dark skin reddening. "I . . . uh . . . mean . . . I thought you were living with Skanea Power-Speaker."

"I was." Nitika touched the Power necklaces about her neck.

Tehanyah's eyes widened. He dipped his head in respect. "Power-Speaker."

No, I'm not! Nitika wanted to protest. But somehow, seeing the wonder of Tehanyah's face, she couldn't say the words.

When she kept silent, Tehanyah continued in a hushed voice: "Maybe you can help us. With . . . That."

"That?" Nitika echoed, bewildered.

Tehanyah glanced about at the darkening forest, and Nitika thought she saw a flicker of fear in his dark eyes. Fear? Tehanyah had never been afraid of anything! "This isn't a good time or place to talk," he said shortly. "Come, let's get back to the lodges before they shut us out."

He wouldn't say another word. Nitika, forcing her weary body on, had to struggle to keep up with his longer stride.

The lodges of the People were suddenly ahead of them, set in a wide clearing and surrounded by a protective palisade of wooden stakes.

"That wall wasn't there before," Nitika said. "Tehanyah, what's going on?"

He shook his head. "Hurry. They're closing the gates."

But Nitika hesitated a moment. "What about Gungosah?" she asked nervously. "Will he let me—"

"He isn't here," Tehanyah cut in. "Come *on*! Eh-hah, Setnak," he shouted, "wait for us!"

They dove inside just as the gates were being pulled shut. Nitika all at once found herself amid too many lodges, too many people, too many curious faces. Surely things had never been so—so crowded when she was a child?

And . . . surely there hadn't been such fear on so many faces? Everyone seemed to be moving closer, surrounding her, eyes wary, and Nitika fought down the urge to turn and run.

Tehanyah hurried to introduce her. "Don't you recognize her? This is Nitika!"

Nobody looked relieved. "How can you be so sure?" somebody muttered.

"It *is* Nitika," Tehanyah protested. "Look, she—"

"It's been a long time," a woman shouted out of the crowd: fat-faced Seela, Nitika realized with a shock of recognition—Seela, who'd always saved a bit of sweet-gum for her when she was a child. Seela, who was now adding coldly, "How do we know what that little girl grew up to be?"

"This might be anyone," a man added sharply. Nitika recognized lean-faced Dakentah the hunter—Dakentah, whose shattered leg Skanea had healed so well he had not the slightest limp. But he obviously didn't recognize her, because he continued, "Maybe . . . someone not even human."

Suddenly all the crowding, all the fear, was too much for Nitika. "Oh, what nonsense!" she shouted at the top of her lungs, and the crowd fell silent. "I *am* Nitika, and I *have* returned! If I was some sort of monster, do you think I would be out when the sun was still shining? Well? Do you? And if I was a creature of evil, how could I possibly be wearing these?"

She held up the Power necklaces so all could see. The crowd buzzed in awe: "Power-Speaker. The old one must be dead; the young one's come back. Come to save us."

"Save you?" Nitika glanced helplessly at Tehanyah. "Save you from what?"

But Tehanyah was moving respectfully aside to make room for a tall, powerfully built man of middle years, his deerskin robe richly embroidered in porcupine quills and beads of shell and gleaming gold, glittering in the last rays of the setting sun. This was Okenhayah, Chief of the People, imposing as ever, though a little more gray threaded his thick braids than Nitika remembered.

"Power-Speaker." Okenhayah gave her a formal dip of his head, equal almost to equal, and all at once Nitika was too scared to argue. "Come," the Chief said. "We must talk."

Nitika had been in the Chief's lodge only once, with Skanea. Then it had seemed a huge, frightening place. Now it was somehow . . . smaller, less imposing, a wicker-and-bark home like any other, smelling cleanly of pine and cooking herbs. Nitika started without thinking for the women's side of the lodge, then remembered just in time that a Power-Speaker was above such rules. She sat instead at Okenhayah's feet, as Skanea had done, hoping she didn't look as nervous as she felt.

The Chief wasted no time. "I imagine old Skanea is dead? A pity; she was a truly wise woman. And you are her replacement, I see. Young though you are."

Nitika struggled to match his brisk tone. "I was in Skanea's training all my life, you know that." There, that wasn't a lie; she wasn't actually claiming to be what she wasn't. "But why do you need a replacement?" she added, daringly. "What about Gungosah?"

"That liar!" Okenhayah straightened angrily. "Oh, I suppose he did have some small Power—but nothing as strong as Skanea's magic, may her spirit forgive us. We made a mistake, choosing him. And he knew it. He went out into the forest one night, swearing he would conjure up true magic, so we'd all respect him. But . . . he never came back."

"He ran away?"

"Who knows?" Okenhayah hesitated, and Nitika saw the fierceness fade from his eyes, leaving him all at once looking old and worn. "The trouble began soon after that. A hunter disappeared: Targah; you probably don't remember him. We . . . found his body in the morning, bloodless and torn as though wild beasts had been at it."

The Chief let out his breath in a weary sigh, and Nitika asked warily: "Why don't you think animals killed him?"

"Because the same thing has happened again and again: a hunter, or a woman gathering fruit, or even a child straying off from the others, anyone who dares linger alone after sundown . . . One by one, they disappear, one by one, their bodies are found in the morning, empty. . . ." Okenhayah stared pleadingly at Nitika. "Power-Speaker, I have gone out there myself, I have tried to hunt down this Killer-by-Night. And I have failed. But you can help us. You must."

No! shrilled a terrified part of Nitika's mind. *Maybe Skanea could have helped you—but I'm not Skanea!* But to Nitika's shock, she heard herself saying, in an almost steady voice, "I will do what I can."

Okenhayah nodded. "I can ask no more." He got to his feet, and Nitika scrambled to hers, wondering with a wildly pounding heart if he was going to ask her to go out into the forest right now. But the Chief said gently, "You've traveled a far way today, haven't you? I can see the weariness on your face. Rest tonight, and have no fear; I shall command that all the People stay safe at home till morning."

Nitika bowed. "Thank you."

"As for where you'll stay . . . Mm. I think Tehanyah's family has room within their lodge." The Chief's eyes were suddenly bright and teasing. "And I'm sure Tehanyah won't mind at all."

"Uh . . . no. I . . . guess not." To her horror, Nitika could feel herself starting to blush. *Stop that!* she told herself fiercely. But no matter how hard she tried, she couldn't forget how handsome Tehanyah had looked, there in the forest. And . . . he had called her pretty . . . For a moment, Nitika found herself wishing that she had never been touched by Power, that she had been left alone to grow up among the lodges as just another girl. Then maybe she and Tehanyah could have . . .

No. What was, was. With a sigh, Nitika followed the Chief out into the open again.

"AH, THERE YOU ARE!" Genesita, Tehanyah's mother, beamed at Nitika, as round-faced and cheerful as the girl remembered. "And how you've grown! My son is right," she added, much to Tehanyah's embarrassment. "You *are* a pretty young woman. And a Power-Speaker, too, and you so young."

Tehanyah coughed politely. "My mother, don't you want to let Nitika find a place to rest?"

"Oh, of course, of course. Come, child, enter our clan lodge in peace."

Nitika had forgotten just how crowded such a lodge could be. After the quiet of the Chief's home—which, by tradition, he shared only with his wives—this long, narrow place seemed to swarm with life. Children rushed up and down the central corridor, squealing, dodging the many cooking fires and the men and women who were preparing food or mending clothing or the partitions of woven reeds that provided some privacy. The air was thick and warm with the smell of smoke and spices and people: Tehanyah's parents, grandparents, cousins, and other kinfolk.

But underneath all the cheerful domesticity, Nitika realized uneasily, was still that faint current of fear.

She froze. Everyone in the lodge seemed to be turning to stare at her, this time with friendly curiosity (and hope? was it hope?) in their eyes. One little boy, too young to be wearing anything other than his own plump brown skin in the lodge's warmth, came scurrying up to her side. As Tehanyah introduced him as Kechi, one of his many cousins, the boy asked eagerly:

"Is it true? Are you really a Power-Speaker? Can you work magic?"

"Kechi!" Genesita was shocked. "It's not polite to question a guest."

Nitika smiled at the wide-eyed boy. "It's all right. And I can work magic, at least a little." She focused her will as Skanea had taught her and reached within herself for a spark of force. It blossomed on her open hand for a moment as a shining golden flame, then vanished back into her inner self as she released it. There was a murmur of satisfaction from the adults: "Power-Speaker, indeed. Just like Skanea."

"Are you satisfied?" Genesita asked Kechi. "Now, be off with you. Nitika, dear, we've made room for you here on the women's side of the lodge, here between me and Aunt Shonea. You remember her, don't you?"

No, Nitika didn't, but she dipped her head courteously to the old woman and received a wide, toothless grin in return.

"You just sit here and rest, dear," continued Genesita, patting Nitika on the arm. "Then come join me and my husband, and that tall, skinny son of mine, for dinner."

At first, Nitika didn't know how to talk to Tehanyah. She just couldn't get used to her old playmate being so . . . handsome now. Oh, and surely her magic would make him uneasy.

But if he was uneasy, Tehanyah hid it very well. He didn't treat her as different at all, teasing her across the central fireplace, joking with her all through the dinner of stewed rabbit and acorn bread, much to the amusement of his parents and the rest of his clan kin, till Nitika was blushing and laughing as she hadn't laughed in all the years away from the People.

I never knew how much I missed all this. I never knew till now how lonely I was.

She had forgotten so much about her own tribe! Oh, the People did respect magic, of course they did, but they weren't afraid of it, not when it was wielded by one of their own. They knew how much a Power-Speaker needed to be reminded that he or she was still human, still in need of human warmth and friendship.

And . . . love? Nitika glanced at Tehanyah across the dying fire. For a moment his eyes were very warm indeed, and the girl wondered at the strange, lovely, bewildering stirring she felt deep within her. For a moment, no one else seemed to exist in the lodge but just the two of them. Then someone coughed, and someone else laughed, and the world rushed back in around them. Tehanyah reddened and looked awkwardly away.

Nitika pretended to be very busy preparing her sleeping-robes. But she couldn't stop herself from wondering: Is this love? Oh, Skanea, you taught me many things. Why didn't you teach me: Is this love?

THAT NIGHT, FOR ALL her weariness, Nitika was unable to fall asleep for what seemed an eternity. She was used to sleeping in Skanea's little hut, not in a long clan lodge like this, with so many people on either side of her. But finally she did drift into slumber . . .

Only to come wide awake again, heart racing. Aie, what was wrong? All around her, the lodge was silent and dark, a warm, friendly sort of darkness that seemed to enfold her in comfort, telling her, You belong here, these are your people, they welcome you. Nitika sighed softly, smiling. The alarm she'd felt must have been only a dream.

But now she found herself unable to get back to sleep. Something was nagging at the edge of her mind, chill as a cold breeze edging under her sleeping robes.

At last the girl gave up. She scrambled back into her clothes as silently as she could, wrapping a blanket about herself for added warmth, and slipped past the hide covering the small, low doorway, out into the night, gasping with shock as the cold air bit at her lungs. It was still a long time till dawn. The sky had cleared, and the stars blazed with painful brightness. Nitika shuddered beneath their chill light, thinking of the nameless terror that hid somewhere out beyond the tribe's protective palisade.

The People trusted her to help them.

"I can't!" Nitika said softly to the night, her breath a plume in the cold.

"You are a Power-Speaker," whispered Skanea's ghost-voice. "In training, in skill, in everything but name: You are a Power-Speaker. Believe."

The air had grown very still. If Nitika opened her senses as Skanea had taught her, she could feel something out there, something bitter, something hating . . . Without conscious thought, the girl moved softly forward, following that faint magical thread.

But then Nitika stopped short, staring. When she had entered with Tehanyah, the palisade gate had been securely latched behind them. Now it stood slightly ajar.

The men who were supposed to be guarding it were curled up in their robes, huddled together against the cold, snoring.

But the sense of that magical, hating, Something was stronger here. And for a long, terrified moment, Nitika wanted very much to turn around and run back to the nice, warm, safe lodge.

To the People who were depending on her.

The People who had no one else to help them.

Nitika bit her lip. There *was* no one else—it was as simple as that. No matter how hard she tried, she couldn't pretend not to be afraid. But she couldn't just give up, either. For her People's sake, she had to find out what waited out there, cold and hating.

Reluctantly, the girl slipped through the gap in the palisade wall and went on. The night was very dark, the starlight cut off by the forest. But Nitika remembered Skanea's lessons, and forced her mind to relax, just *so*.

Ah, now she could see! Now she could find her way by the light of magic: a faint blue-white glow invisible to anyone not trained in Power.

Heart racing, Nitika walked on through the forest as silently as she could, letting magic guide her. The sense of chill, chill hatred grew stronger with every step, whispering of death in the air all around her.

But whoever—whatever—is doing the hating doesn't seem to know I'm here.

So Nitika dared steal a little closer, one hand closed tightly about her Power necklaces. Carefully she parted two bushes and saw a rocky little gully. Rain, flooding, and time had washed the earth out from under a stand of vast oak trees, leaving a network of roots exposed to form a living cave.

No, wait now. Those weren't only roots. Nitika blinked, and looked again. Woven into them was a lodge of sorts, an ugly little hut of branches and bits of bark, so sunken into the ground that the girl could understand why even the most skillful of the People hadn't found it. The aura of hatred was so powerful here that Nitika clenched her teeth to keep them from chattering. But she didn't see anything frightening. Maybe if she edged her way around to face the front of the lodge . . . ?

A body lay stretched out limply on the ground. A second, shadowy figure bent over it, a man's figure, surely, though there somehow seemed to be something very wrong with it. For a wild moment, Nitika couldn't figure out what the man meant to do. Then she saw his teeth glint, the sharp teeth of a predator-beast about to strike. She saw the face of his prey:

It was Tehanyah!

He must have been the one who'd left the gate ajar, he must have come out here while she'd slept—but why? Why?

No time to worry about it. Nitika remembered the Chief's description of "bodies found in the morning, empty . . ." and forgot all caution. She plunged forward into the open. The startled predator-man whirled to face her, raging, his eyes hot with hatred for all that lived. But despite those terrible eyes, something in the contorted face brought a surge of memory to Nitika's mind, of the time when Skanea had taken her from the People and left behind the other, victorious Power-Speaker . . .

"Gungosah . . . ?"

WAS IT TRULY HE? Or, rather, was it still he . . . ? Those alien, alien eyes . . . The Power necklaces were suddenly ablaze with magic, nearly burning her skin, reacting to his presence as they never had to anyone before, and every nerve in her body seemed to be reacting with them, tight with alarm.

And all at once Nitika knew what was wrong: Every living thing had a faint shimmering of light playing about it, visible to those who were trained to see such things, a reflection of the life force within. But no life light played about Gungosah, no life at all.

"No . . ." Nitika said slowly, struggling to keep her voice from shaking. "You're not Gungosah, are you? Not—not anymore. You're . . . dead."

"No! Not dead!" the once-Gungosah shouted. "I am . . . changed. Better. More powerful." He frowned, blinking, then continued, in a more nearly human tone, "I knew you once. Yes . . . a brat-child, running after that—Skanea! Thinking herself so strong, so mighty. Now *I* am the mighty one!" The dead eyes stared. "After she left, folk dared to mock me. They called me a liar, a sham. But I went into the forest alone, I made conjurings of Power—I drew Darkness to me and made it mine."

Nitika winced. "You called up Darkness, and it killed you," she corrected softly. Had she just seen Tehanyah stir? Was he regaining consciousness? She must keep the once-Gungosah distracted. "The Darkness possessed your body. It turned you into Dead-Alive, Life-Stealer."

"Not Life-Stealer, little one. Magic-Stealer." The once-Gungosah gave a sharp, humorless grin. "Oh, yes, I kill, I take blood, I must feed to exist. But every life bears within it a touch of magic, no matter how slight, you know that. With each kill, I steal that body's magic, make it part of me."

He knows, Nitika realized suddenly. *The part of him that's still Gungosah knows he's dead. And it's driven him insane.*

Somehow that seemed much more terrible than if he'd become a true Dead-Alive, a mindless predator.

The Dead-Alive continued savagely, "At last I shall have all the magic, all. I shall be the greatest, most terrible of Power-Speakers." His mad, terrible eyes, hot as the heart of hatred, held her transfixed. Desperately, Nitika tore her gaze away, even as the once-Gungosah shrieked, "*And now I shall take your magic, too!*"

He lunged. But suddenly Tehanyah came to life, grabbing at the once-Gungosah's leg. The being went crashing to the ground, and Tehanyah leaped on top of him, yelling: "Nitika! Run!"

But then the Dead-Alive lurched to his feet, throwing Tehanyah aside without effort. The young man crashed into the trunk of a tree and crumpled, and the once-Gungosah whirled to him, teeth bared.

"Stop it!" Nitika screamed. "Get away from him!"

But those were only empty words. Tehanyah was going to die, while she stood by and did nothing.

I can't *do anything! I'm only an apprentice!*

Tehanyah was going to die for her sake. Just as Skanea had died—

"*But . . . that's not true,*" Nitika protested. "*She didn't die for me, she just—died. It wasn't my fault.*"

"You are Power-Speaker now," whispered Skanea's spirit-voice. "Believe!"

Tehanyah was going to die, and all love and joy with him—

"No!" Nitika shouted fiercely, and sudden sharp fire blazed up within her. "This shall not be!" She laughed in wild delight as magic woke within her, aching to be used. *Oh, Skanea, you were right all along, I do have Power! I was only afraid to try and fail*—"Dead-Alive, you shall not have him!"

And she spoke her Power free. The Dead-Alive staggered back beneath the sudden force of it, eyes wide with alarm. He tried to lunge at Nitika, but Power blocked his leap. He tried to run, but Power caught him, tossed him back. With a savage hiss, the once-Gungosah darted aside, diving into his lodge. Nitika called Fire into being, the ever-feeding, never-fed, hurled it forth from her will. The lodge blazed up with white-hot magical flame.

Panting, Nitika waited, never daring to blink. At her side, Tehanyah stirred, sitting up.

"Is it over?" he asked warily.

From the heart of the blaze came an eerie howl. Man had entered, blood-red fox raced out: Dead-Alive transformed.

"Look out! Don't let him escape!"

Nitika caught the fox in her blanket, wrestling it to the ground, struggling to hold it pinned. The fox writhed within her grasp, yelping, shrieking:

Fox had been snared, death-white owl soared up: Dead-Alive transformed. Hunter-quick, Tehanyah hurled a stone. The owl shrieked as it was struck and fell back into the heart of the flames.

Owl had fallen, cloud of ashes whirled up: Dead-Alive transformed one last time. Nitika hurled her blanket over it, forcing it back into the flames, holding blanket and ashes and flames together with her song till at last the final embers died.

Warily, the girl stirred the ashes with a branch.

Nothing remained. The Dead-Alive was gone; what had been left of Gungosah was free.

All at once, Nitika was too weary to stand. As she crumpled, she heard Tehanyah's sharp cry of alarm, but she was already sliding helplessly into sleep.

SHE WOKE TO EARLY-MORNING grayness. She also woke to find herself in Tehanyah's arms. As soon as he felt her stir, the young man hastily let her go, his face red.

"Are . . . are you all right?" he asked.

Nitika nodded. "Skanea warned me. Power-Speaking can be truly exhausting—Oh, Tehanyah, it's true, I *am* a Power- Speaker!"

He blinked. "I never thought you weren't."

"You don't understand. I . . . What were you doing out here?"

"I . . . uh . . . was trying to protect you. I remember leaving the lodge. But after that . . ." Tehanyah shook his head. "Gungosah must have worked a spell on me, because the next thing I remember is waking up with him about to take a bite." He gave Nitika a rueful grin. "A fine protector I turned out to be!"

If you hadn't been in danger, Nitika thought, *I might never have accepted Power.* But of course she couldn't say that. "If you hadn't thrown that stone at the owl, the Dead-Alive would have escaped."

"Then we're both heroes, eh?"

Nitika looked up into the warmth of his eyes and all at once wanted to laugh aloud in joy. "I suppose we are." But then a sudden disconcerting idea struck her.

"Tehanyah, you must promise me something: Never let me get as—as conceited as Gungosah."

"Oh, no danger of that!" Tehanyah scrambled up, holding out his hands to her. She let him pull her to her feet, which he did with such enthusiasm that she was flung into his arms, held so close that their lips were nearly touching. "Unless," Tehanyah added breathlessly, "it's conceit over being a certain someone's sweetheart."

"Tehanyah! I'm being serious."

"So am I. I was, right from the instant I met you in the forest." But then, embarrassed, he hastily let her go. "You were talking about using your magic, weren't you? Don't worry. I promise, I'll never let Power get the better of you."

"It . . . really doesn't bother you that I'm a—a Power-Speaker?"

Would she ever be able to say that word without stumbling?

Tehanyah looked at her in genuine surprise. "Why should it? Some people are born hunters, some are weavers, and some—"

"Are Power-Speakers."

"Exactly. Now, let's get back to the lodges before they come looking for us."

But Nitika hesitated for a moment, smiling, almost sure she heard the fading whisper of Skanea's spirit: "You're on your own now, girl. Live, be wise, be happy."

I will, she answered joyfully, *oh, I will, indeed.*

THE WORDS OF GURU

Cyril M. Kornbluth

Yesterday, when I was going to meet Guru in the woods, a man stopped me and said: "Child, what are you doing out at one in the morning? Does your mother know where you are? How old are you, walking around this late?"

I looked at him, and saw that he was white-haired, so I laughed. Old men never see; in fact men hardly see at all. Sometimes young women see part, but men rarely ever see at all. "I'm twelve on my next birthday," I said. And then, because I would not let him live to tell people, I said, "and I'm out this late to see Guru."

"Guru?" he asked. "Who is Guru? Some foreigner, I suppose? Bad business mixing with foreigners, young fellow. Who is Guru?"

181

So I told him who Guru was, and just as he began talking about cheap magazines and fairy tales I said one of the words that Guru taught me and he stopped talking. Because he was an old man and his joints were stiff he didn't crumple up but fell in one piece, hitting his head on the stone. Then I went on.

Even though I'm going to be only twelve on my next birthday, I know many things that old people don't. And I remember things that other boys can't. I remember being born out of darkness, and I remember the noises that people made about me. Then when I was two months old I began to understand that the noises meant things like the things that were going on inside my head. I found out that I could make the noises too, and everybody was very much surprised. "Talking!" they said, again and again. "And so very young! Clara, what do you make of it?" Clara was my mother.

And Clara would say: "I'm sure I don't know. There never was any genius in my family, and I'm sure there was none in Joe's." Joe was my father.

Once Clara showed me a man I had never seen before, and told me that he was a reporter—that he wrote things in newspapers. The reporter tried to talk to me as if I were an ordinary baby; I didn't even answer him, but just kept looking at him until his eyes fell and he went away. Later Clara scolded me and read me a little piece in the reporter's newspaper that was supposed to be funny—about the reporter asking me very complicated questions and me answering with baby noises. It was not true, of course. I didn't say a word to the reporter, and he didn't ask me even one of the questions.

I heard her read the little piece, but while I listened I was watching the slug crawling on the wall. When Clara was finished I asked her: "What is that grey thing?"

She looked where I pointed, but couldn't see it. "What grey thing, Peter?" she asked. I had her call me by my whole name, Peter, instead of anything silly like Petey. "What grey thing?"

"It's as big as your hand, Clara, but soft. I don't think it has any bones at all. It's crawling up, but I don't see any face on the topwards side. And there aren't any legs."

I think she was worried, but she tried to baby me by putting her hand on the wall and trying to find out where it was. I called out whether she was right or left of the thing. Finally she put her hand right through the slug. And then I realized that she really couldn't see it, and didn't believe it was there. I stopped talking about it then and only asked her a few days later: "Clara, what do you call a thing which one person can see and another person can't?"

"An illusion, Peter," she said. "If that's what you mean." I said nothing, but let her put me to bed as usual, but when she turned out the light and went away I waited a little while and then called out softly. "Illusion! Illusion!"

At once Guru came for the first time. He bowed, the way he always has since, and said: "I have been waiting."

"I didn't know that was the way to call you," I said.

"Whenever you want me I will be ready. I will teach you, Peter—if you want to learn. Do you know what I will teach you?"

"If you will teach me about the grey thing on the wall," I said, "I will listen. And if you will teach me about real things and unreal things I will listen."

"These things," he said thoughtfully, "very few wish to learn. And there are some things that nobody ever wished to learn. And there are some things that I will not teach."

Then I said: "The things nobody has ever wished to learn I will learn. And I will even learn the things you do not wish to teach."

He smiled mockingly. "A master has come," he said half-laughing. "A master of Guru."

That was how I learned his name. And that night he taught me a word which would do little things, like spoiling food.

From that day to the time I saw him last night he has not changed at all, though now I am as tall as he is. His skin is still as dry and shiny as ever it was, and his face is still bony, crowned by a head of very coarse, black hair.

WHEN I WAS TEN years old I went to bed one night only long enough to make Joe and Clara suppose I was fast asleep. I left in my place something which appears when you say one of the words of Guru and went down the drainpipe outside my window. It always was easy to climb down and up, ever since I was eight years old.

I met Guru in Inwood Hill Park. "You're late," he said.

"Not too late," I answered. "I know it's never too late for one of these things."

"How do you know?" he asked sharply. "This is your first."

"And maybe my last," I replied. "I don't like the idea of it. If I have nothing more to learn from my second than my first I shan't go to another."

"You don't know," he said. "You don't know what it's like—the voices, and the bodies slick with unguent, leaping flames; mind-filling ritual! You can have no idea at all until you've taken part."

"We'll see," I said. "Can we leave from here?"

"Yes," he said. Then he taught me the word I would need to know, and we both said it together.

The place we were in next was lit with red lights, and I think that the walls were of rock. Though of course there was no real seeing there, and so the lights only seemed to be red, and it was not real rock.

As we were going to the fire one of them stopped us. "Who's with you?" she asked, calling Guru by another name. I did not know that he was also the person bearing that name, for it was a very powerful one.

He cast a hasty, sidewise glance at me and then said: "This is Peter of whom I have often told you."

She looked at me then and smiled, stretching out her oily arms. "Ah," she said, softly, like the cats when they talk at night to me. "Ah, this is Peter. Will you come to me when I call you, Peter? And sometimes call for me—in the dark—when you are alone?"

"Don't do that!" said Guru, angrily pushing past her. "He's very young—you might spoil him for his work."

She screeched at our backs: "Guru and his pupil—fine pair! Boy, he's no more real than I am—you're the only real thing here!"

"Don't listen to her," said Guru. "She's wild and raving. They're always tight-strung when this time comes around."

We came near the fires then, and sat down on rocks. They were killing animals and birds and doing things with their bodies. The blood was being collected in a basin of stone, which passed through the crowd. The one to my left handed it to me. "Drink," she said, grinning to show me her fine, white teeth. I swallowed twice from it and passed it to Guru.

When the bowl had passed all around we took off our clothes. Some, like Guru, did not wear them, but many did. The one to my left sat closer to me, breathing heavily at my face. I moved away. "Tell her to stop, Guru," I said. "This isn't part of it, I know."

Guru spoke to her sharply in their own language, and she changed her seat, snarling.

Then we all began to chant, clapping our hands and beating our thighs. One of them rose slowly and circled about the fires in a slow pace, her eyes rolling wildly. She worked her jaws and flung her arms about so sharply that I could hear the elbows crack. Still shuffling her feet against the rock floor she bent her body backwards down to her feet. Her belly muscles were bands nearly standing out from her skin, and the oil rolled down her body and legs. As the palms of her hands touched the ground, she collapsed in a twitching heap and began to set up a thin wailing noise against the steady chant and hand beat that the rest of us were keeping up. Another of them did the same as the first, and we chanted louder for her and still louder for the third. Then, while we still beat our hands and thighs, one of them took up the third, laid her across the altar, and made her ready with a stone knife. The fire's light gleamed off the chipped edge of obsidian. As her blood drained down the groove, cut as a gutter into the rock of the altar, we stopped our chant and the fires were snuffed out.

But still we could see what was going on, for these things were, of course, not happening at all—only seeming to happen, really, just as all the people and things there only seemed to be what they were. Only I was real. That must be why they desired me so.

As the last of the fires died Guru excitedly whispered: "The Presence!" He was very deeply moved.

From the pool of blood from the third dancer's body there issued the Presence. It was the tallest one there, and when it spoke its voice was deeper, and when it commanded its commands were obeyed.

"Let blood!" it commanded, and we gashed ourselves with flints. It smiled and showed teeth bigger and sharper and whiter than any of the others.

"Make water!" it commanded, and we all spat on each other. It flapped its wings and rolled its eyes, which were bigger and redder than any of the others.

"Pass flame!" it commanded, and we breathed smoke and fire on our limbs. It stamped its feet, let blue flames roar from its mouth, and they were bigger and wilder than any of the others.

Then it returned to the pool of blood and we lit the fires again. Guru was staring straight before him; I tugged his arm. He bowed as though we were meeting for the first time that night.

"What are you thinking of?" I asked. "We shall go now."

"Yes," he said heavily. "Now we shall go." Then we said the word that had brought us there.

The first man I killed was Brother Paul, at the school where I went to learn the things that Guru did not teach me.

It was less than a year ago, but it seems like a very long time. I have killed so many times since then.

"You're a very bright boy, Peter," said the brother.

"Thank you, brother."

"But there are things about you that I don't understand. Normally I'd ask your parents but—I feel that they don't understand either. You were an infant prodigy, weren't you?"

"Yes, brother."

"There's nothing very unusual about that—glands, I'm told. You know what glands are?"

Then I was alarmed. I had heard of them, but I was not certain whether they were the short, thick green men who wear only metal or the things with many legs with whom I talked in the woods.

"How did you find out?" I asked him.

"But Peter! You look positively frightened, lad! I don't know a thing about them myself, but Father Frederick does. He has whole books about them, though I sometimes doubt whether he believes them himself."

"They aren't good books, brother," I said. "They ought to be burned."

"That's a savage thought, my son. But to return to your own problem—"

I could not let him go any further knowing what he did about me. I said one of the words Guru taught me and he looked at first very surprised and then seemed to be in great pain. He dropped across his desk and I felt his wrist to make sure, for I had not used that word before. But he was dead.

There was a heavy step outside and I made myself invisible. Stout Father Frederick entered, and I nearly killed him too with the word, but I knew that that would be very curious. I decided to wait, and went through the door as Father Frederick bent over the dead monk. He thought he was asleep.

I went down the corridor to the book-lined office of the stout priest and, working quickly, piled all his books in the center of the room and lit them with my breath. Then I went down to the schoolyard and made myself visible again when there was nobody looking. It was very easy. I killed a man I passed on the street the next day.

There was a girl named Mary who lived near us. She was fourteen then, and I desired her as those in the Cavern out of Time and Space had desired me.

So when I saw Guru and he had bowed, I told him of it, and he looked at me in great surprise. "You are growing older, Peter," he said.

"I am, Guru. And there will come a time when your words will not be strong enough for me."

He laughed. "Come, Peter," he said. "Follow me if you wish. There is something that is going to be done—" He licked his thin, purple lips and said: "I have told you what it will be like."

"I shall come," I said. "Teach me the word." So he taught me the word and we said it together.

The place we were in next was not like any of the other places I had been to before with Guru. It was No-place. Always before there had been the seeming passage of time and matter, but here there was not even that. Here Guru and the others cast off their forms and were what they were, and No-place was the only place where they could do this.

It was not like the Cavern, for the Cavern had been out of Time and Space, and this place was not enough of a place even for that. It was No-place.

What happened there does not bear telling, but I was made known to certain ones who never departed from there. All came to them as they existed. They had not color or the seeming of color, or any seeming of shape.

There I learned that eventually I would join with them; that I had been selected as the one of my planet who was to dwell without being forever in that No-place.

Guru and I left, having said the word.

"Well?" demanded Guru, staring me in the eye.

"I am willing," I said. "But teach me one word now—"

"Ah," he said grinning. "The girl?"

"Yes," I said. "The word that will mean much to her."

Still grinning, he taught me the word.

Mary, who had been fourteen, is now fifteen and what they call incurably mad.

LAST NIGHT I SAW Guru again and for the last time. He bowed as I approached him. "Peter," he said warmly.

"Teach me the word," said I.

"It is not too late."

"Teach me the word."

"You can withdraw—with what you master you can master also this world. Gold without reckoning; sardonyx and gems, Peter! Rich crushed velvet—stiff, scraping, embroidered tapestries!"

"Teach me the word."

"Think, Peter, of the house you could build. It could be of white marble, and every slab centered by a winking ruby. Its gate could be of beaten gold within and without and it could be built about one slender tower of carven ivory, rising mile after mile into the turquoise sky. You could see the clouds float underneath your eyes."

"Teach me the word."

"Your tongue could crush the grapes that taste like melted silver. You could hear always the song of the bulbul and the lark that sounds like the dawnstar made musical. Spikenard that will bloom a thousand thousand years could be ever in your nostrils. Your hands could feel the down of purple Himalayan swans that is softer than a sunset cloud."

"Teach me the word."

"You could have women whose skin would be from the black of ebony to the white of snow. You could have women who would be as hard as flints or as soft as a sunset cloud."

"Teach me the word."

Guru grinned and said the word.

Now, I do not know whether I will say that word, which was the last that Guru taught me, today or tomorrow or until a year has passed.

It is a word that will explode this planet like a stick of dynamite in a rotten apple.

LOST BOYS

Orson Scott Card

I've worried for a long time about whether to tell this story as fiction or fact. Telling it with made-up names would make it easier for some people to take. Easier for me, too. But to hide my own lost boy behind some phony made-up name would be like erasing him. So I'll tell it the way it happened, and to hell with whether it's easy for either of us.

Kristine and the kids and I moved to Greensboro on the first of March, 1983. I was happy enough about my job—I just wasn't sure I wanted a job at all. But the recession had the publishers all panicky, and nobody was coming up with advances large enough for me to take a decent amount of time writing a novel. I suppose I could whip out seventy-five thousand words of junk fiction every month and publish them under a half dozen pseudonyms, or something, but it seemed to Kristine and me that we'd do better in the long run if I got a job to ride out the recession. Besides, my Ph.D. was down the toilet. I'd been doing good work at Notre Dame, but when I had to take out a few weeks in the middle of a semester to finish *Hart's Hope*, the English Department was about as understanding as you'd expect from people who prefer their authors dead or domesticated. Can't feed your family? So sorry. You're a writer? Ah, but not one that anyone's written a scholarly essay about. So long, boy-oh!

So sure, I was excited about my job, but moving to Greensboro also meant that I had failed. I had no way of knowing that my career as a fiction writer wasn't over. Maybe I'd be editing and writing books about computers for the rest of my life. Maybe fiction was just a phase I had to go through before I got a *real* job.

Greensboro was a beautiful town, especially to a family from the western desert. So many trees that even in winter you could hardly tell there was a town at all. Kristine and I fell in love with it at once. There were local problems, of course—people bragged about Greensboro's crime rate and talked about racial tension and what-not—but we'd just come from a depressed northern industrial town with race riots in the high schools, so to us this was Eden. There were rumors that several child disappearances were linked to some serial kidnapper, but this was the era when they started putting pictures of missing children on milk cartons—those stories were in every town.

It was hard to find decent housing for a price we could afford. I had to borrow from the company against my future earnings just to make the move. We ended up in the ugliest house on Chinqua Drive. You know the house—the one with cheap wood siding in a

neighborhood of brick, the one-level rambler surrounded by split-levels and two-stories. Old enough to
be shabby, not old enough to be quaint. But it had a
big fenced yard and enough bedrooms for all the kids
and for my office, too—because we hadn't given up on
my writing career, not yet, not completely.

The little kids—Geoffrey and Emily—thought the
whole thing was really exciting, but Scotty, the oldest, he
had a little trouble with it. He'd already had kindergarten and half of first grade at a really wonderful private
school down the block from our house in South Bend.
Now he was starting over in mid-year, losing all his
friends. He had to ride a school bus with strangers. He
resented the move from the start, and it didn't get better.

Of course, *I* wasn't the one who saw this. *I* was at
work—and I very quickly learned that success at Compute! Books meant giving up a few little things like
seeing your children. I had expected to edit books written by people who couldn't write. What astonished me
was that I was editing books about computers written by
people who couldn't *program.* Not all of them, of course,
but enough that I spent far more time rewriting pro-
grams so they made sense—so they even *ran*—than I did
fixing up people's language. I'd get to work at 8:30 or
9:00, then work straight through till 9:30 or 10:30 at
night. My meals were Three Musketeers bars and potato
chips from the machine in the employee lounge. My
exercise was typing. I met deadlines, but I was putting on
a pound a week and my muscles were all atrophying and
I saw my kids only in the mornings as I left for work.

Except Scotty. Because he left on the school bus at
6:45 and I rarely dragged out of bed until 7:30, during
the week I never saw Scotty at all.

The whole burden of the family had fallen on Kristine. During my years as a freelancer from 1978 to 1983, we'd got used to a certain pattern of life, based on the fact that Daddy was *home*. She could duck out and run some errands, leaving the kids, because I was home. If one of the kids was having discipline problems, I was there. Now if she had her hands full and needed something from the store; if the toilet clogged; if the Xerox jammed, then she had to take care of it herself, somehow. She learned the joys of shopping with a cartful of kids. Add to this the fact that she was pregnant and sick half of the time, and you can understand why sometimes I couldn't tell whether she was ready for sainthood or the funny farm.

The finer points of child-rearing just weren't within our reach at that time. She knew that Scotty wasn't adapting well at school, but what could she do? What could I do?

Scotty had never been the talker Geoffrey was—he spent a lot of time just keeping to himself. Now, though, it was getting extreme. He would answer in monosyllables, or not at all. Sullen. As if he were angry, and yet if he was, he didn't know it or wouldn't admit it. He'd get home, scribble out his homework (did they give homework when *I* was in first grade?), and then just mope around.

If he had done reading, or even watched TV, then we wouldn't have worried so much. His little brother Geoffrey was already a compulsive reader at age five, and Scotty used to be. But now Scotty'd pick up a book and set it down again without reading it. He didn't even follow his mom around the house or anything. She'd see him sitting in the family room, go in and change the sheets on the beds, put away a load of clean clothes, and then come back in and find him sitting in the same place, his eyes open, staring at *nothing*.

I tried talking to him. Just the conversation you'd expect:

"Scotty, we know you didn't want to move. We had no choice."

"Sure. That's O.K."

"You'll make new friends in due time."

"I know."

"Aren't you ever happy here?"

"I'm O.K."

Yeah, right.

But we didn't have *time* to fix things up, don't you see? Maybe if we'd imagined this was the last year of Scotty's life, we'd have done more to right things, even if it meant losing the job. But you never know that sort of thing. You always find out when it's too late to change anything.

And when the school year ended, things *did* get better for a while.

For one thing, I saw Scotty in the mornings. For another thing, he didn't have to go to school with a bunch of kids who were either rotten to him or ignored him. And he didn't mope around the house all the time. Now he moped around outside.

At first Kristine thought he was playing with our other kids, the way he used to before school divided them. But gradually she began to realize that Geoffrey and Emily always played together, and Scotty almost never played with them. She'd see the younger kids with their squirtguns or running through the sprinklers or chasing the wild rabbit who lived in the neighborhood, but Scotty was never with them. Instead, he'd be poking a twig into the tent-fly webs on the trees, or digging around at the open skirting around the bottom of the house that kept animals out of the crawl space. Once or twice a week he'd come in so dirty that Kristine had to heave him into the tub, but it didn't reassure her that Scotty was acting normally.

ON JULY 28TH, KRISTINE went to the hospital and gave birth to our fourth child. Charlie Ben was born having a seizure, and stayed in intensive care for the first weeks of his life as the doctors probed and poked and finally figured out that they didn't know what was wrong. It was several months later that somebody uttered the words "cerebral palsy," but our lives had already been transformed by then. Our whole focus was on the child in the greatest need—that's what you *do*, or so we thought. But how do you measure a child's need? How do you compare those needs and decide who deserves the most?

When we finally came up for air, we discovered that Scotty had made some friends. Kristine would be nursing Charlie Ben, and Scotty'd come in from outside and talk about how he'd been playing army with Nicky or how he and the guys had played pirate. At first she thought they were neighborhood kids, but then one day when he talked about building a fort in the grass (I didn't get many chances to mow), she happened to remember that she'd seen him building that fort all by himself. Then she got suspicious and started asking questions. Nicky who? I don't know, Mom. Just Nicky. Where does he live? Around. I don't know. Under the house.

In other words, imaginary friends.

How long had he known them? Nicky was the first, but now there were eight names—Nicky, Van, Roddy, Peter, Steve, Howard, Rusty, and David. Kristine and I had never heard of anybody having more than one imaginary friend.

"The kid's going to be more successful as a writer than I am," I said. "Coming up with eight fantasies in the same series."

Kristine didn't think it was funny. "He's so *lonely*, Scott," she said. "I'm worried that he might go over the edge."

It *was* scary. But if he was going crazy, what then? We even tried taking him to a clinic, though I had no faith at all in psychologists. Their fictional explanations of human behavior seemed pretty lame, and their cure rate was a joke—a plumber or barber who performed at the same level as a psychotherapist would be out of business in a month. I took time off work to drive Scotty to the clinic every week during August, but Scotty didn't like it and the therapist told us nothing more than what we already knew—that Scotty was lonely and morose and a little bit resentful and a little bit afraid. The only difference was that she had fancier names for it. We were getting a vocabulary lesson when we needed help. The only thing that seemed to be helping was the therapy we came up with ourselves that summer. So we didn't make another appointment.

Our homegrown therapy consisted of keeping him from going outside. It happened that our landlord's father, who had lived in our house right before us, was painting the house that week, so that gave us an excuse. And I brought home a bunch of videogames, ostensibly to review them for *Compute!*, but primarily to try to get

Scotty involved in something that would turn his imagination away from these imaginary friends.

It worked. Sort of. He didn't complain about not going outside (but then, he never complained about anything), and he played the videogames for hours a day. Kristine wasn't sure she loved *that*, but it was an improvement—or so we thought.

Once again, we were distracted and didn't pay much attention to Scotty for a while. We were having insect problems. One night Kristine's screaming woke me up. Now, you've got to realize that when Kristine screams, that means everything's pretty much O.K. When something really terrible is going on, she gets cool and quiet and *handles* it. But when it's a little spider or a huge moth or a stain on a blouse, then she screams. I expected her to come back into the bedroom and tell me about this monstrous insect she had to hammer to death in the bathroom.

Only this time, she didn't stop screaming. So I got up to see what was going on. She heard me coming—I was up to 230 pounds by now, so I sounded like Custer's whole cavalry—and she called out, "Put your shoes on first!"

I turned on the light in the hall. It was hopping with crickets. I went back into my room and put on my shoes.

After enough crickets have bounced off your naked legs and squirmed around in your hands you stop wanting to puke—you just scoop them up and stuff them into a garbage bag. Later you can scrub yourself for six hours before you feel clean and have nightmares about little legs tickling you. But at the time your mind goes numb and you just do the job.

The infestation was coming out of the closet in the boys' room, where Scotty had the top bunk and Geoffrey slept on the bottom. There were a couple of crickets in Geoff's bed, but he didn't wake up even as we changed his top sheet and shook out his blanket. Nobody but us even saw the crickets. We found the crack in the back of the closet, sprayed Black Flag into it, and then stuffed it with an old sheet we were using for rags.

Then we showered, making jokes about how we could have used some seagulls to eat up our invasion of crickets, like the Mormon pioneers got in Salt Lake. Then we went back to sleep.

It wasn't just crickets, though. That morning in the kitchen Kristine called me again: There were dead June bugs about three inches deep in the window over the sink, all down at the bottom of the space between the regular glass and the storm window. I opened the window to vacuum them out, and the bug corpses spilled all over the kitchen counter. Each bug made a nasty little rattling sound as it went down the tube toward the vacuum filter.

The next day the window was three inches deep again, and the day after. Then it tapered off. Hot fun in the summertime.

We called the landlord to ask whether he'd help us pay for an exterminator. His answer was to send his father over with bug spray, which he pumped into the crawl space under the house with such gusto that we had to flee the house and drive around all that Saturday until a late afternoon thunderstorm blew away the stench and drowned it enough that we could stand to come back.

Anyway, what with that and Charlie's continuing problems, Kristine didn't notice what was happening with the videogames at all. It was on a Sunday afternoon that I happened to be in the kitchen, drinking a Diet coke, and heard Scotty laughing out loud in the family room.

That was such a rare sound in our house that I went and stood in the door to the family room, watching him play. It was a great little videogame with terrific animation: Children in a sailing ship, battling pirates who kept trying to board, and shooting down giant birds that tried to nibble away the sail. It didn't look as mechanical as the usual videogame, and one feature I really liked was the fact that the player wasn't alone— there were other computer-controlled children helping the player's figure to defeat the enemy.

"Come on, Sandy!" Scotty said. "Come on!" Whereupon one of the children on the screen stabbed the pirate leader through the heart, and the pirates fled.

I couldn't wait to see what scenario this game would move to then, but at that point Kristine called me to come and help her with Charlie. When I got back, Scotty was gone, and Geoffrey and Emily had a different game in the Atari.

Maybe it was that day, maybe later, that I asked Scotty what was the name of that game about children on a pirate ship. "It was just a game, Dad," he said.

"It's got to have a name."

"I don't know."

"How do you find the disk to put it in the machine?"

"I don't know." And he sat there staring past me and I gave up.

Summer ended. Scotty went back to school. Geoffrey started kindergarten, so they rode the bus together. More important, things settled down with the newborn, Charlie—there wasn't a cure for cerebral palsy, but at least we knew the bounds of his condition. He wouldn't get *worse*, for instance. He also wouldn't get well. Maybe he'd talk and walk someday, and maybe he wouldn't. Our job was just to stimulate him enough that if it turned out he wasn't retarded, his mind would develop even though his body was so drastically limited. It was doable. The fear was gone, and we could breathe again.

Then, in mid-October, my agent called to tell me that she'd pitched my Alvin Maker series to Tom Doherty at TOR Books, and Tom was offering enough of an advance that we could live. That plus the new contract for *Ender's Game,* and I realized that for us, at least, the recession was over. For a couple of weeks I stayed on at Compute! Books, primarily because I had so many projects going that I couldn't just leave them in the lurch. But then I looked at what the job was doing to my family and to my body, and I realized the price was too high. I gave two weeks' notice, figuring to wrap up the projects that only I knew about. In true paranoid fashion, they refused to accept the two weeks—they had me clean my desk out that afternoon. It left a bitter taste, to have them act so churlishly, but what the heck. I was free. I was home.

You could almost feel the relief. Geoffrey and Emily went right back to normal; I actually got acquainted with Charlie Ben; Christmas was coming (I start playing Christmas music when the leaves turn) and all was right with the world. Except Scotty. Always except Scotty.

It was then that I discovered a few things that I simply hadn't known. Scotty never played any of the videogames I'd brought home from *Compute!* I knew that because when I gave the games back, Geoff and Em complained bitterly—but Scotty didn't even know what the missing games *were*. Most important, that game about kids in a pirate ship wasn't there. Not in the games I took back, and not in the games that belonged to us. Yet Scotty was still playing it.

He was playing one night before he went to bed. I'd been working on *Ender's Game* all day, trying to finish it before Christmas. I came out of my office about the third time I heard Kristine say, "Scotty, go to bed *now!*"

For some reason, without yelling at the kids or beating them or anything, I've always been able to get them to obey when Kristine couldn't even get them to acknowledge her existence. Something about a fairly deep male voice—for instance, I could always sing insomniac Geoffrey to sleep as an infant when Kristine couldn't. So when I stood in the doorway and said, "Scotty, I think your mother asked you to go to bed," it was no surprise that he immediately reached up to turn off the computer.

"*I'll* turn it off," I said. "Go!"

He still reached for the switch.

"Go!" I said, using my deepest voice-of-God tones.

He got up and went, not looking at me.

I walked to the computer to turn it off, and saw the animated children, just like the ones I'd seen before. Only they weren't on a pirate ship, they were on an old steam locomotive that was speeding along a track. What a game, I thought. The single-sided Atari disks didn't even hold a 100K, and here they've got two complete scenarios and all this animation and—

And there wasn't a disk in the disk drive.

That meant it was a game that you upload and then remove the disk, which meant it was completely RAM resident, which meant all this quality animation fit into a mere 48K. I knew enough about game programming to regard that as something of a miracle.

I looked around for the disk. There wasn't one. So Scotty had put it away, I thought. Only I looked and looked and couldn't find any disk that I didn't already know.

I sat down to play the game—but now the children were gone. It was just a train. Just speeding along. And the elaborate background was gone. It was the plain blue screen behind the train. No tracks, either. And then no train. It just went blank, back to the ordinary blue. I touched the keyboard. The letters I typed appeared on the screen. It took a few carriage returns to realize what was happening—the Atari was in memo-pad mode. At first I thought it was a pretty terrific copy-protection scheme, to end the game by putting you into a mode where you couldn't access memory, couldn't do anything without turning off the machine, thus erasing the program code from RAM. But then I realized that a company that could produce a game so good, with such tight code, would surely have some kind of sign-off when the game ended. And why did it end? Scotty hadn't touched the computer after I told him to stop. I didn't touch it, either. Why did the children leave the screen? Why did the train disappear? There was no way the computer could "know" that Scotty was through playing, especially since the game *had* gone on for a while after he walked away.

Still, I didn't mention it to Kristine, not till after everything was over. She didn't know anything about computers then except how to boot up and get Word-Star on the Altos. It never occurred to her that there was anything weird about Scotty's game.

It was two weeks before Christmas when the insects came again. And they shouldn't have—it was too cold outside for them to be alive. The only thing we could figure was that the crawl space under our house stayed warmer or something. Anyway, we had another exciting night of cricket-bagging. The old sheet was still wadded up in the crack in the closet—they were coming from under the bathroom cabinet this time. And the next day it was daddy-long-legs spiders in the bathtub instead of June bugs in the kitchen window.

"Just don't tell the landlord," I told Kristine. "I couldn't stand another day of that pesticide."

"It's probably the landlord's father *causing* it," Kristine told me. "Remember he was here painting when it happened the first time? And today he came and put up the Christmas lights."

We just lay there in bed chuckling over the absurdity of that notion. We had thought it was silly but kind of sweet to have the landlord's father insist on putting up Christmas lights for us in the first place. Scotty went out and watched him the whole time. It was the first time he'd ever seen lights put up along the edge of the roof— I have enough of a case of acrophobia that you couldn't get me on a ladder high enough to do the job, so our house always went undecorated except the tree lights you could see through the window. Still, Kristine and I are both suckers for Christmas kitsch. Heck, we even play the Carpenters' Christmas album. So we thought it was great that the landlord's father wanted to do that for us. "It was my house for so many years," he said. "My wife and I always had them. I don't think this house'd look *right* without lights."

He was such a nice old coot anyway. Slow, but still strong, a good steady worker. The lights were up in a couple of hours.

Christmas shopping. Doing Christmas cards. All that stuff. We were busy.

Then one morning, only about a week before Christmas, I guess, Kristine was reading the morning paper and she suddenly got all icy and calm—the way she does when something *really* bad is happening. "Scott, read this," she said.

"Just *tell* me," I said.

"This is an article about missing children in Greensboro."

I glanced at the headline: CHILDREN WHO WON'T BE HOME FOR CHRISTMAS. "I don't want to hear about it," I said. I can't read stories about child abuse or kidnappings. They make me crazy. I can't sleep afterward. It's always been that way.

"You've got to," she said. "Here are the names of the little boys who've been reported missing in the last three years. Russell DeVerge, Nicholas Tyler—"

"What are you getting at?"

"Nicky. Rusty. David. Roddy. Peter. Are these names ringing a bell with you?"

I usually don't remember names very well. "No."

"Steve, Howard, Van. The only one that doesn't fit is the last one. Alexander Booth. He disappeared this summer."

For some reason the way Kristine was telling me this was making me very upset. *She* was so agitated about it, and she wouldn't get to the point. "So *what?*" I demanded.

"Scotty's imaginary friends," she said.

"Come on," I said. But she went over them with me—she had written down all the names of his imaginary friends in our journal, back when the therapist asked us to keep a record of his behavior. The names matched up, or seemed to.

"Scotty must have read an earlier article," I said. "It must have made an impression on him. He's always been an empathetic kid. Maybe he started identifying with them because he felt—I don't know, like maybe he'd been abducted from South Bend and carried off to Greensboro." It sounded really plausible for a moment there—the same moment of plausibility that psychologists live on.

Kristine wasn't impressed. "This article says that it's the first time anybody's put all the names together in one place."

"Hype. Yellow journalism."

"Scott, he got *all* the names right."

"Except one."

"I'm so relieved."

But I wasn't. Because right then I remembered how I'd heard him talking during the pirate videogame. Come on Sandy. I told Kristine. Alexander, Sandy. It was as good a fit as Russell and Rusty. He hadn't matched a mere eight out of nine. He'd matched them all.

You can't put a name to all the fears a parent feels, but I can tell you that I've never felt any terror for myself that compares to the feeling you have when you watch your two-year-old run toward the street, or see your baby go into a seizure, or realize that somehow there's a connection between kidnappings and your child. I've never been on a plane seized by terrorists or had a gun pointed to my head or fallen off a cliff, so maybe there are worse fears. But then, I've been in a spin on a snowy freeway, and I've clung to the handles of my airplane seat while the plane bounced up and down in mid-air, and still those weren't like what I felt then, reading the whole article. Kids who just disappeared. Nobody saw anybody pick up the kids. Nobody saw anybody lurking around their houses. The kids just didn't come home from school, or played outside and never came in when they were called. Gone. And Scotty knew all their names. Scotty had played with them in his imagination. How did he know who they were? Why did he fixate on these lost boys?

We watched him, that last week before Christmas. We saw how distant he was. How he shied away, never let us touch him, never stayed with a conversation. He was aware of Christmas, but he never asked for anything, didn't seem excited, didn't want to go shopping. He didn't even seem to sleep. I'd come in when I was heading for bed—at one or two in the morning, long after he'd climbed up into his bunk—and he'd be lying there, all his covers off, his eyes wide open. His insomnia was even worse than Geoffrey's. And during the day, all Scotty wanted to do was play with the computer or hang around outside in the cold. Kristine and I didn't know what to do. Had we already lost him somehow?

We tried to involve him with the family. He wouldn't go Christmas shopping with us. We'd tell him to stay inside while we were gone, and then we'd find him outside anyway. I even unplugged the computer and hid all the disks and cartridges, but it was only Geoffrey and Emily who suffered—I still came into the room and found Scotty playing his impossible game.

He didn't ask for anything until Christmas Eve.

Kristine came into my office, where I was writing the scene where Ender finds his way out of the Giant's Drink problem. Maybe I was so fascinated with computer games for children in that book because of what Scotty was going through—maybe I was just trying to pretend that computer games made sense. Anyway, I still know the very sentence that was interrupted when she spoke to me from the door. So very calm. So very frightened.

"Scotty wants us to invite some of his friends in for Christmas Eve," she said.

"Do we have to set extra places for imaginary friends?" I asked.

"They aren't imaginary," she said. "They're in the back yard, waiting."

"You're kidding," I said. "It's *cold* out there. What kind of parents would let their kids go outside on Christmas Eve?"

She didn't say anything. I got up and we went to the back door together. I opened the door.

There were nine of them. Ranging in age, it looked like, from six to maybe ten. All boys. Some in shirt sleeves, some in coats, one in a swimsuit. I've got no memory for faces, but Kristine does. "They're the ones," she said softly, calmly, behind me. "That one's Van. I remembered him."

"Van?" I said.

He looked up at me. He took a timid step toward me.

I heard Scotty's voice behind me. "Can they come in, Dad? I told them you'd let them have Christmas Eve with us. That's what they miss the most."

I turned to him. "Scotty, these boys are all reported missing. Where have they been?"

"Under the house," he said.

I thought of the crawl space. I thought of how many times Scotty had come in covered with dirt last summer.

"How did they get there?" I asked.

"The old guy put them there," he said. "They said I shouldn't tell anybody or the old guy would get mad and they never wanted him to be mad at them again. Only I said it was O.K., I could tell you."

"That's right," I said.

"The landlord's father," whispered Kristine.

I nodded.

"Only how could he keep them under there all this time? When does he feed them? When—"

She already knew that the old guy didn't feed them. I don't want you to think Kristine didn't guess that immediately. But it's the sort of thing you deny as long as you can, and even longer.

"They can come in," I told Scotty. I looked at Kristine. She nodded. I knew she would. You don't turn away lost children on Christmas Eve. Not even when they're dead.

Scotty smiled. What that meant to us—Scotty smiling. It had been so long. I don't think I really saw a smile

like that since we moved to Greensboro. Then he called
out to the boys. "It's O.K.! You can come in!"

Kristine held the door open, and I backed out of
the way. They filed in, some of them smiling, some of
them too shy to smile. "Go on into the living room," I
said. Scotty led the way. Ushering them in, for all the
world like a proud host in a magnificent new mansion.
They sat around on the floor. There weren't many presents, just the ones from the kids; we don't put out the
presents from the parents till the kids are asleep. But
the tree was there, lighted, with all our homemade decorations on it—even the old needlepoint decorations
that Kristine made while lying in bed with desperate
morning sickness when she was pregnant with Scotty,
even the little puff-ball animals we glued together for
that first Christmas tree in Scotty's life. Decorations
older than he was. And not just the tree—the whole
room was decorated with red and green tassels and little
wooden villages and a stuffed Santa hippo beside a
wicker sleigh and a large chimney-sweep nutcracker and
anything else we hadn't been able to resist buying or
making over the years.

We called in Geoffrey and Emily, and Kristine
brought in Charlie Ben and held him on her lap while I
told the stories of the birth of Christ—the shepherds
and the wise men, and the one from the Book of
Mormon about a day and a night and a day without
darkness. And then I went on and told what Jesus lived
for. About forgiveness for all the bad things we do.

"Everything?" asked one of the boys.

It was Scotty who answered. "No!" he said. "Not
killing."

Kristine started to cry.

"That's right," I said. "In our church we believe that God doesn't forgive people who kill on purpose. And in the New Testament Jesus said that if anybody ever hurt a child, it would be better for him to tie a huge rock around his neck and jump into the sea and drown."

"Well, it *did* hurt, Daddy," said Scotty. "They never told me about that."

"It was a secret," said one of the boys. Nicky, Kristine says, because she remembers names and faces.

"You should have told me," said Scotty. "I wouldn't have let him touch me."

That was when we knew, really knew, that it was too late to save him, that Scotty, too, was already dead.

"I'm sorry, Mommy," said Scotty. "You told me not to play with them anymore, but they were my friends, and I wanted to be with them." He looked down at his lap. "I can't even cry anymore. I used it all up."

It was more than he'd said to us since we moved to Greensboro in March. Amid all the turmoil of emotions I was feeling, there was this bitterness: All this year, all our worries, all our efforts to reach him, and yet nothing brought him to speak to us except death.

But I realized now it wasn't death. It was the fact that when he knocked, we opened the door, that when he asked, we let him and his friends come into our house that night. He had trusted us, despite all the distance between us during that year, and we didn't disappoint him. It was that trust that brought us one last Christmas Eve with our boy.

But we didn't try to make sense of things that night. They were children, and needed what children long for on a night like that. Kristine and I told them Christmas stories and we told about Christmas traditions we'd heard of in other countries and other times, and gradually they warmed up until every one of the boys told us all about his own family's Christmases. They were good memories. They laughed, they jabbered, they joked. Even though it was the most terrible of Christmases, it was also the best Christmas of our lives, the one in which every scrap of memory is still precious to us, the perfect Christmas in which being together was the only gift that mattered. Even though Kristine and I don't talk about it directly now, we both remember it. And Geoffrey and Emily remember it, too. They call it "the Christmas when Scotty brought his friends." I don't think they ever really understood, and I'll be content if they never do.

Finally, though, Geoffrey and Emily were both asleep. I carried each of them to bed as Kristine talked to the boys, asking them to help us. To wait in our living room until the police came, so they could help us stop the old guy who stole them away from their families and their futures. They did. Long enough for investigating officers to get there and see them, long enough for them to hear the story Scotty told.

Long enough for them to notify the parents. They came at once, frightened because the police had dared not tell them more over the phone than this: that they were needed in a matter concerning their lost boy. They came: with eager, frightened eyes they stood on our doorstep, while a policeman tried to help them understand. Investigators were bringing ruined bodies out from under the house—there was no hope. And yet if they came inside, they would see that cruel Providence was also kind, and *this* time there would be what so many other parents had longed for but never had: a chance to say good-bye. I will tell you nothing of the scenes of joy and heartbreak inside our home that night—those belong to other families, not to us.

Once their families came, once the words were spoken and the tears were shed, once the muddy bodies were laid on canvas on our lawn and properly identified from the scraps of clothing, then they brought the old man in handcuffs. He had our landlord and a sleepy lawyer with him, but when he saw the bodies on the lawn he brokenly confessed, and they recorded his confession. None of the parents actually had to look at him; none of the boys had to face him again.

But they knew. They knew that it was over, that no more families would be torn apart as theirs—as ours—had been. And so the boys, one by one, disappeared. They were there, and then they weren't there. With that the other parents left us, quiet with grief and awe that such a thing was possible, that out of horror had come one last night of mercy and of justice; both at once.

Scotty was the last to go. We sat alone with him in our living room, though by the lights and talking we were aware of the police still doing their work outside. Kristine and I remember clearly all that was said, but what mattered most to us was at the very end.

"I'm sorry I was so mad all the time last summer," Scotty said. "I knew it wasn't really your fault about moving and it was bad for me to be so angry but I just was."

For him to ask *our* forgiveness was more than we could bear. We were full of far deeper and more terrible regrets, we thought, as we poured out our remorse for all that we did or failed to do that might have saved his life. When we were spent and silent at last, he put it all in proportion for us. "That's O.K. I'm just glad that you're not mad at me." And then he was gone.

We moved out that morning before daylight; good friends took us in, and Geoffrey and Emily got to open the presents they had been looking forward to for so long. Kristine's and my parents all flew out from Utah and the people in our church joined us for the funeral. We gave no interviews to the press; neither did any of the other families. The police told only of the finding of the bodies and the confession. We didn't agree to it; it's as if everybody who knew the whole story also knew that it would be wrong to have it in headlines in the supermarket.

Things quieted down very quickly. Life went on. Most people don't even know we had a child before Geoffrey. It wasn't a secret. It was just too hard to tell. Yet, after all these years, I thought it *should* be told, if it could be done with dignity, and to people who might understand. Others should know how it's possible to find light shining even in the darkest place. How even as we learned of the most terrible grief of our lives, Kristine and I were able to rejoice in our last night with our first-born son, and how together we gave a good Christmas to those lost boys, and they gave as much to us.

AFTERWORD

In August 1988 I brought this story to the Sycamore Hill Writers Workshop. That draft of the story included a disclaimer at the end, a statement that the story was fiction, that Geoffrey is my oldest child and that no landlord of mine has ever done us harm. The reaction of the other writers at the workshop ranged from annoyance to fury.

Karen Fowler put it most succinctly when she said, as best as I can remember her words, "By telling this story in first person with so much detail from your own life, you've appropriated something that doesn't belong to you. You've pretended to feel the grief of a parent who has lost a child, and you don't have a right to feel that grief."

When she said that, I agreed with her. While this story had been rattling around in my imagination for years, I had only put it so firmly in first person the autumn before, at a Halloween party with the students of Watauga College at Appalachian State. Everybody was trading ghost stories that night, and so on a whim I tried out this one; on a whim I made it highly personal, partly because by telling true details from my own life I spared myself the effort of inventing a character, partly because ghost stories are most powerful when the audience half-believes they might be true. It worked better than any tale I'd ever told out loud, and so when it came time to write it down, I wrote it the same way.

Now, though, Karen Fowler's words made me see it in a different moral light, and I resolved to change it forthwith. Yet the moment I thought of revising the story, of stripping away the details of my own life and replacing them with those of a made-up character, I felt a sick dread inside. Some part of my mind was rebelling against what Karen said. No, it was saying, she's wrong, you *do* have a right to tell this story, to claim this grief.

I knew at that moment what this story was *really* about, why it had been so important to me. It wasn't a simple ghost story at all; I hadn't written it just for fun. I should have known—I never write anything just for fun. This story wasn't about a fictional eldest child named "Scotty." It was about my real-life youngest child, Charlie Ben.

Charlie, who in the five and a half years of his life has never been able to speak a word to us. Charlie, who could not smile at us until he was a year old, who could not hug us until he was four, who still spends his days and nights in stillness, staying wherever we put him, able to wriggle but not to run, able to call out but not to speak, able to understand that he cannot do what his brother and sister do, but not to ask us why. In short, a child who is not dead and yet can barely taste life despite all our love and all our yearning.

Yet in all the years of Charlie's life, until that day at Sycamore Hill, I had never shed a single tear for him, never allowed myself to grieve. I had worn a mask of calm and acceptance so convincing that I had believed it myself. But the lies we live will always be confessed in the stories that we tell, and I am no exception. A story that I had fancied was a mere lark, a dalliance in the quaint old ghost-story tradition, was the most personal, painful story of my career—and, unconsciously, I had confessed as much by making it by far the most autobiographical of all my works.

Months later, I sat in a car in the snow at a cemetery in Utah, watching a man I dearly love as he stood, then knelt, then stood again at the grave of his eighteen-year-old daughter. I couldn't help but think of what Karen had said: truly I had no right to pretend that I was entitled to the awe and sympathy we give to those who have lost a child. And yet I knew that I couldn't leave this story untold, for that would also be a kind of lie. That was when I decided on this compromise: I would publish the story as I knew it had to be written, but then I would write this essay as an afterword, so that you would know exactly what was true and what was not true in it. Judge it as you will; this is the best that I know how to do.

AUTHORS' BIOGRAPHIES

Suzy McKee Charnas is a multi-award-winning author whose latest novel is *The Conqueror's Child*. She has garnered acclaim for her unusual look at the tropes of science fiction and fantasy, often turning the genres upside down. A former volunteer for the Peace Corps, she has also taught economic history, English, and history, and she has served as an instructor at several writer's workshops, including Clarion East and West. Charnas lives in Albuquerque, New Mexico.

Larry Segriff is an author and editor working in the science fiction, fantasy, and mystery fields. His recent novels include *The Four Magics* (coauthored with William R. Forstchen), *Spacer Dreams*, and *Alien Dreams*, with a fourth novel in progress. He has also coedited several anthologies, including *Murder Most Irish* and *Cat Crimes Through Time*. He lives in Green Bay, Wisconsin, with his wife and two daughters.

Charles de Lint is a full-time writer and musician who presently makes his home in Ottawa, Ontario, Canada, with his wife MaryAnn Harris, an artist and musician. His most recent books are *Somewhere to Be Flying* and the single-author collection entitled *Moonlight and Vines*. For more information on his work, visit his Web site at www.cyberus.ca/~cdl.

J. Sheridan Le Fanu (1814–1873) was an Irish writer who spent much of his life as the owner of various newspapers and journals in Dublin. Primarily known as a writer of supernatural fiction, he is best known for the stories written in the seven years before his death, of which "The Child That Went with the Fairies" is one.

Al Sarrantonio's writing covers a wide range of territory that includes horror, mystery, western, and science fiction. His short tales of horror, which have appeared in *Whispers*, *The Horror Show*, and the *Shadows* anthologies, helped to define contemporary dark fantasy. His novels include *The Worms*, *Campbell Wood*, *October*, *House Haunted*, and the science fiction werewolf story "Moonbane." Sarrantonio has served as an officer of the Horror Writers of America and coedited the anthology *100 Hair-Raising Little Horror Stories*.

Lee Hoffman was born in Chicago but grew up in Savannah, Georgia. She subsequently spent time on ranches in Colorado, worked briefly as a horse trader in Kansas, then moved to New York City, where, as she puts it, "I fell in with evil companions and eventually began writing for a living." Although most of her books are westerns, she has written science fiction/horror and a historical romance novel set during the Civil War. Hoffman returned to the South—Florida this time—and has been spending her days attending science fiction conventions, dabbling in handicrafts, and watching old movies.

Fritz Leiber (1910–1992) is widely considered one of the founding fathers of sword and sorcery fiction with his elegantly witty tales of Fafhrd and the Grey Mouser ranking beside Robert Howard's Conan tales for their impact. His science fiction is no less memorable, having won the Hugo Award for his novels *The Wanderer* and *The Big Time*. Other novels of his include *Conjure Wife*, a tale of modern-day witchcraft and the uses it has in the world of academia, and *Our Lady of Darkness*, which won the World Fantasy Award. A fifty-year retrospective of his short fiction, *The Leiber Chronicles*, was published by Dark Harvest Press.

Nina Kiriki Hoffman has been pursuing a writing career for fifteen years and has sold more than 150 stories; two short-story collections; two novels—*The Thread That Binds the Bones*, winner of the Bram Stoker Award for best first novel, and *The Silent Strength of Stones*; one novella, *Unmasking;* and one collaborative young-adult novel with Tad Williams, *Child of an Ancient City*.

Josepha Sherman is a fantasy writer and folklorist whose latest novels are *Highlander: The Captive Soul* and *Son of Darkness*. Her most recent folklore volume is *Merlin's Kin: World Tales of the Hero Magicians*. Her short fiction has appeared in numerous anthologies, including *Battle Magic, Dinosaur Fantastic*, and *The Shimmering Door*. She lives in Riverdale, New York.

Cyril M. Kornbluth (1923–1958) primarily collaborated with Frederik Pohl on novels of social science fiction, but it is his shorter stories that are considered his more excellent work. Often combining a humorous look at social conventions with a strange sense of piercing the veils of common perception, many of his stories straddle the boundary between fantasy and science fiction. Other noted works of Kornbluth include "The Silly Season" and "The Mindworm."

Orson Scott Card, best known for his Nebula and Hugo Award–winning science fiction novels *Ender's Game* and *Speaker for the Dead*, is also an accomplished fantasy and horror writer. Among his other achievements are two Locus Awards, a Hugo Award for nonfiction, and a World Fantasy Award. Currently, he is working on the Tales of Alvin Maker series, which chronicles the history of an alternate nineteenth-century America where magic works. The Alvin Maker series, like the majority of his work, deals with messianic characters and their influence on the world around them. His short fiction has been collected in the anthology *Maps in a Mirror*.

COPYRIGHTS AND PERMISSIONS